PRAISE FOR *TELEVISION*

"Standing between the pamphlet and the fable, *Television* is written with constant humor. In this novel, each of us will find an echo of our own relations with TV, in all its ambiguity."

—Françoise Giroud, *Le Figaro*

"Some essayists have analyzed with seriousness the crisis of representation—and thus the crisis of civilization—that started with the continuous attack of virtual pictures to which we are subjected. Jean-Philippe Toussaint describes it in a novelistic way with a comic effectiveness, and an exemplary criticism."

—Pierre Lepape, *Le Monde*

"There is not much going on in *Television*. . . . There is no apparent reason (for giving up watching TV). Despite this or thanks to it, it is very easy to get caught in the screen. Therefore we need to resist it, just as we could resist *Television*. But we can also be seduced by Jean-Philippe Toussaint's style—clear, with a distant irony and a kind of humor, which is most of the time inserted between parentheses—and by his thoughts about our relations to the television; thoughts, which are more entertaining and funny than sensational."

—Frédéric Mairy

TELEVISION

Jean-Philippe Toussaint

~TRANSLATION BY JORDAN STUMP~
~AFTERWORD BY WARREN MOTTE~

DALKEY ARCHIVE PRESS

NORMAL · LONDON

First published as *La Télévision* by Les Éditions de Minuit, 1997
Copyright © 1997 by Jean-Philippe Toussaint
Translation © 2004 by Jordan Stump
Afterword © 2004 by Warren Motte

First edition, 2004

Library of Congress Cataloging-in-Publication Data available
ISBN 1-56478-372-3

Ouvrage publié avec le concours du Ministère français chargé de la Culture – Centre National du Livre.
[This Work has been published thanks to the French Ministry of Culture – National Book Center.]

Partially funded by a grant from the Illinois Arts Council, a state agency.

Dalkey Archive Press is a nonprofit organization located in Milner Library at
Illinois State University and distributed in the UK by
Turnaround Publisher Services Ltd. (London).

www.centerforbookculture.org

Printed on permanent/durable acid-free paper and bound in the United States of America.

TELEVISION

I quit watching television. I gave it up cold turkey, once and for all, never to watch another show, not even sports. I stopped a little more than six months ago, in late July, just after the end of the Tour de France. I'd quietly watched the delayed broadcast of the Tour's last stage in my Berlin apartment, like everyone else—the Champs-Élysées stage, ending in a tremendous sprint won by the Uzbek Abdujaparov—and then I stood up and turned off the set. I can clearly picture myself at that moment, the very simple gesture I made, my arm fluidly extending as it had a thousand times before, my finger on the button, the picture imploding and disappearing from the screen. It was over. I never watched television again.

The TV set is still sitting in the living room, dark and forsaken. I haven't touched it since. I'm sure it still works. I could find out with a touch of the button. It's a standard model, sitting on a lacquered wooden stand made up of two elements, a shelf and a pedestal, the pedestal in the form of a thin black book, upright and open, like a silent reproach. The screen is an indefinable color, dark and uninviting, I wouldn't call it green, and very slightly convex. On one side a little compartment houses the various controls. An antenna sprouts from the top, its two stems making a V, a bit like the twin antennae of a crayfish, and offering the same sort of handle for any-one who might want to pick it up and drop it into a pot of boiling water to rid himself of it even more completely.

I spent the summer alone in Berlin. Delon, whom I live with, went off to Italy on vacation with the two children, my son and the not-yet-born baby we were expecting—a little girl, in my opinion. I assumed it was a little girl because the gynecologist couldn't find a male member on the sonogram (and when there's no male member, it's often a little girl, I'd explained).

Not that television ever held an especially important place in my life. No. On average, I watched maybe two hours a day (maybe less, but I'd rather err on the side of generosity, and not try to puff myself up with a virtuously low estimate). Apart from major sporting events, which I always watched with pleasure, and of course the news and the occasional election-night special, I never watched much of anything on television. As a matter of principle and pleasure, I never watched movies on television, for instance (just as I don't read books in Braille). For that matter, although I never tried it, I was always quite sure I could give up watching television anytime, just like that, without suffering in the least, without the slightest ill effect—in short, that there was no way I could be considered dependent.

And yet, over the previous few months, I'd noticed a slight deterioration in my day-to-day habits. I spent most afternoons at home, unshaved, dressed in a wonderfully comfortable old wool sweater, watching television for three or four hours at a stretch, half-reclining on the couch, taking it easy, a little like a cat in its bed, my feet bare, my hand cradling my privates. Just being myself, in other words. Thus, this year, unlike years past, I followed the French Tennis Open on television from beginning to end. At first it was only a match here and there, but then, with the quarterfinals, I began to take a real interest in the outcome, or so I explained to Delon to justify my long inactive afternoons in front of the set. Most of these afternoons I was alone in the apartment, but sometimes the cleaning woman was there too, ironing my shirts beside me in the living room, mute with contained indignation. On the worst days, the broadcasts started at noon and didn't end until after nightfall. I emerged from those sessions nauseous and numbed, my mind empty, my legs limp, my eyes bleary. I went off and took a shower, letting the warm water pour over my face for many minutes. I was wiped out for the rest of the evening, and, however reluctant I was to admit it, there was no getting around the fact that, ever since I'd very gradually begun to turn forty years old, I was no longer physically up to five sets of tennis.

Apart from that I did nothing. By doing nothing, I mean doing nothing impulsive or mechanical, nothing dictated by habit or laziness. By doing nothing, I mean doing only the essential, thinking, reading, listening to music, making love, going for walks, going to the pool, gathering mushrooms. Doing nothing, contrary to what people rather simplistically imagine, is a thing that requires method and discipline, concentration, an open mind. I swim five-hundred meters every day nowadays, at a rate of two kilometers per hour, a leisurely pace I admit, equaling exactly twenty pool-lengths every fifteen minutes, which is to say eighty pool-lengths in an hour. But high performance isn't my goal. I swim slowly, like an old woman (albeit without the bathing-cap), my mind ideally empty, focused on my body and its movement, carefully observing my motions and their timing, my mouth half-open as I exhale, blowing a spray of little lapping bubbles over the surface. Afloat in the blue-tinged pool, my limbs surrounded by limpid water, I slowly reach forward and push the water behind me with long strokes, my knees drawing level with my hips; then, as my arms slowly extend once more, my legs simultaneously push the water behind them in one coordinated and synchronized movement. In the end, I rank swimming very highly among the pleasures that life has to offer us, having in the past somewhat underestimated it and placed it rather far behind physical love, which was until now my favorite activity, apart from thinking, of course. I do in fact very much like making love (on more than one account), and, without going into my own personal style in that domain, which is in any case closer to the sensual quietude of a leisurely breast-stroke pool length than to the surging, swaggering outburst of a four-hundred meter butterfly race, I will say above all that making love brings me an immense inner equilibrium, and that, the embrace at an end, as I lie dreamily on my back on the soft sheets, savoring the simple companionship of the moment, I find myself in an irrepressible good mood, which appears on my face as a slight, unexpected smile, and something gleaming in my eye, something light-hearted and knowing. And it turns out that swimming brings me the same sort of satisfaction, that same bodily plenitude, slowly spreading to the mind, like a wave, little by little, giving birth to a smile.

And so I realized, busy as I was doing nothing, that I no longer had time to watch television.

Television offers the spectacle not of reality, although it has all the appearances of reality (on a smaller scale, I would say—I don't know if you've ever watched television), but rather of its representation. It is true that television's apparently neutral representation of reality, in color and in two dimensions, seems at first glance more trustworthy, authentic, and credible than the more refined and much more indirect sort of representation painters use to create an image of reality in their works; but when artists represent reality, they do so in order to take in the outside world and grasp its essence, while television, if it represents reality, does so in and of itself, unintentionally you might say, through sheer technical determinism, or incontinence. But the fact that television offers a familiar and immediately recognizable image of reality does not mean that its images and reality can be considered equivalent. Unless you believe that reality has to resemble its representation in order to be real, there's no reason to see a Renaissance master's portrait of a young man as any less faithful a vision of reality than the apparently incontestable video image of an anchorman, world-famous in his own country, reading the news on a TV screen.

A Renaissance painting's illusion of reality, rooted in colors and pigments, in oils and brushstrokes, in delicate retouches with the brush or even the finger, or a simple smearing of the slightly damp linseed oil paste with the side of the thumb, the illusion that you have before you something living, flesh or hair, fabric or drapery, that you stand before a complex, human person, with his flaws and weaknesses, someone with a history, with his own nobility, his sensitivity, his gaze—just how many square millimeters of paint does it take to create the force of that gaze, looking down through the centuries?—is by its nature fundamentally different from the illusion offered by television when it represents reality, the purely mechanical result of an uninhabited technology.

I'd decided to spend the summer alone in Berlin to devote myself to my study of Titian Vecellio. For several years now I'd been planning a vast essay on the relationship between political power and the arts. Little by little, my focus had narrowed to sixteenth-century Italy, and more particularly to Titian Vecellio and Emperor Charles V; in the end, I'd chosen the apocryphal story of the paintbrush—according to which Charles V bent down in Titian's studio to pick up a paintbrush that had slipped from the painter's hands—as my monograph's emblematic center and the source of its title, *The Paintbrush*. I'd begun a sabbatical from my university post at the start of the year, so I could concentrate on my writing. Meanwhile, having learned of a private foundation in Berlin with a mission to aid researchers of my stripe, I'd applied for a grant. I put together a file with a detailed description of my project, carefully emphasizing that my research would absolutely require a visit to Augsburg, where Charles V had resided from 1530 until I no longer know what year (oh, dates), and where, most significantly, Titian had painted several of the finest portraits of Charles V, the large equestrian portrait now in the Prado, for instance, as well as the seated Charles V in Munich's Alte Pinakothek, his face pale and sad, a glove in his hand. It goes without saying that a stay in Augsburg might have been extraordinarily fruitful and profitable for my work, but at the same time I was perfectly prepared to concede that this project on Titian Vecellio wasn't really as specifically German as I'd sought to suggest in the skillfully-crafted little essay attached to my grant application, and that at bottom it was no more difficult, for example, to travel to Augsburg from Paris than from Berlin. Munich would have been ideal. In the end, though, I got the grant (which goes to show), and the three of us went off to Germany. At the beginning of July, Delon left for a vacation in Italy with the two children, one in her hand, the other in her stomach (eminently practical when you're always loaded down with an insane number of suitcases and handbags, as she is), and I'd accompanied the three of them to the airport. My job was to carry the tickets. I can clearly see myself in the great hall, heading toward the massive departures board, tickets in hand, looking up, comparing the one to the other with an uncertain air. Then I came back to Delon, who was waiting beside her baggage cart, and said—I don't know if every word I spoke during this stay in Berlin will be reported so faithfully here—"Gate 28." "Are you sure?" Delon asked. A nagging little doubt suddenly crept into my mind. "Gate 28, yes" (I'd gone back to check again). We kissed at some length before going our separate ways, and I bid them farewell by the check-in counter at gate 28. I gently passed my hand over my son's head and under my Delon's sweater, tenderly touching her stomach, and I watched them step through the simple little triumphal arch of the metal detector. "Good-bye, good-bye," my son signified with a wave of his hand (and now I wanted to cry: that's just like me).

Back home again, I did some straightening up, carefully tidying my study in preparation for the work to come (I was planning to launch into my writing very early the next morning). I began by clearing off the tall black bookshelf, where a great many papers had accumulated since my arrival in Berlin: mail and bills, assorted calling cards, various unclassified documents related to my work, some coins and old concert tickets, and a great stack of newspaper clippings in French and German that I'd been saving to read later, in tranquillity. I must have carefully cut all these articles out, one after another, as the days went by; I can well imagine myself clipping away, sitting at my desk, then standing to go and put them on a shelf with the others, to be thrown away at some later date, if not to be read at some point. Once I'd completely emptied the armoire, I began to sort through my clippings, sitting cross-legged on the floor of my study, the distended sleeves of my old wool sweater pushed up to the elbows. With a large plastic trash bag lying open nearby, I took the articles one by one from the piles around me and began to skim through them a little, naturally, as one does (sometimes, in my archival zeal, I even went so far as to stand up and get a pen from my desk to annotate a paragraph, or underline a sentence, or date a clipping), then tossed them into the bag, preserving only a few particularly interesting specimens, rigorously selected, for later perusal; with delighted anticipatory relish, I went and laid these on the nightstand in my bedroom once I'd finished my tidying. Then

I quickly swept up, opened the balcony door to air out my study, went and gave the rugs a good shake in the open air, and got rid of the briefcase and portfolio that were sitting on top of my bed. With these various preliminaries completed, I set my alarm clock to 6:45, and, checking one last time to be sure that everything in the apartment was in order, that everything was ready in my study, my desk neat, a ream of blank paper beside the computer, my books and notes properly arranged and ready for use, I very gently closed the study door, made my way to the living room, sat down on the couch, and turned on the television.

Some time before, as if caught up in some sordid intoxication, I'd taken to turning on the TV in the evening and watching everything there was to see, my mind perfectly empty, never choosing any particular program, simply watching everything that came my way, the movement, the glimmering lights, the variety. At the time I didn't quite realize just what was happening to me, but looking back, I see that short-lived period of overindulgence as a classic forerunner of the radical decision that was to come, as if, to make a clean break, you first had to go through such a phase of excessive consumption. In the meantime, I spent hours every evening motionless before the screen, my gaze fixed, bathed in the ever-shifting light of the scene changes, gradually submerged by the flood of images illuminating my face, the long parade of images blindly addressed to everyone at once and no one in particular, each channel being only another strand in the vast web of electromagnetic waves daily crashing down over the world. Powerless to react, I nevertheless understood full well that I was debasing myself in these long sessions before the screen, unable to drop the remote, mechanically and frenetically changing channels in a quest for sordid and immediate pleasures, swept up in that vain inertia, that insatiable spiral, searching for ever more vileness, still more sadness.

Everywhere it was the same undifferentiated images, without margins or titles, without explanation, raw, incomprehensible, noisy and bright, ugly, sad, aggressive and jovial, syncopated, all equivalent, it was stereotypical American series, it was music videos, it was songs in English, it was game shows, it was documentaries, it was film scenes removed from their context, excerpted, it was excerpts, it was a snatch of song, it was lively, the audience clapping along in time, it was politicians sitting around a table, it was a roundtable, it was the circus, it was acrobatics, it was a game show, it was joy, unbelieving stunned laughter, hugs and tears, it was a new car being won live and in color, lips trembling with emotion, it was documentaries, it was World War II, it was a funeral march, it was columns of German prisoners trudging along a roadside, it was the liberation of the death camps, it was piles of bones on the ground, it was in all languages and on more than thirty-two channels, it was in German, it was mostly in German, everywhere it was violence and gunshots, it was bodies lying in the street, it was news, it was floods, it was football, it was game shows, it was a host with his papers before him, it was a spinning wheel that everyone in the studio was watching with heads raised, nine, it was nine, it was applause, it was commercials, it was variety shows, it was debates, it was animals, it was a man rowing in the studio, an athlete rowing and the hosts looking on with anxious expressions, sitting at a round table, a chronometer superimposed over the picture, it was images of war, the sound and framing oddly uneven, as if filmed on the fly, the picture shaking, the camera-man must have been running too, it was people running down a street and someone shooting at them, it was a woman falling, it was a woman who'd been hit, a woman of about fifty lying on the sidewalk, her slightly shabby gray coat gaping half open, her stock-ing torn, she'd been wounded in the thigh and she was crying out, simply crying out, screaming simple cries of horror because her thigh had been ripped open, it was the cries of that woman in pain, she was calling for help, it wasn't fiction, two or three men came back and lifted her onto the curb, the shots were still coming, it was archival footage, it was news, it was commercials, it was new cars gently snaking along idyllic roads in the light of the setting sun, it was a rock concert, it was series, it was classical music, it was a special news bulletin, it was ski-jumping, the crouching skier pushing off down the ramp, serenely letting himself glide onto the jump and leaving the world behind, motionless in midair, he was flying, he was flying, it was magnificent, that frozen body bending forward, motionless and immutable in midair. It was over. It was over: I turned off the television and lay still on the couch.

One of the principal characteristics of a turned-on television is that it artificially keeps us in a state of continual alertness, bombard-ing us with an endless stream of signals, all sorts of little stimuli, visual and aural, whose goal is to arouse our attention and keep our minds watchful. Provoked by these signals, the mind gathers its forces to think, but the television has already moved on to something else, to whatever comes next, new stimuli, new signals, just as strident as the ones before; soon, refusing to be held in this vigilant state by the television's unending stream of deceptive signals, recalling the disappointments of the previous moments and no doubt eager not to be fooled again, the mind begins to anticipate the true nature of the signals it is receiving, and so, rather than once again mustering its forces for reflection, it relaxes them, releases them, and lets itself drift over the tide of images set before it. Thus, as if anesthetized from having been so little stimulated even as it has been so incessantly appealed to, the human mind remains essentially passive before a television screen. Increasingly indifferent to the images it receives, it soon ceases to react at all when new signals are sent its way, knowing that to react would only mean once again falling prey to television's deceptions. Because television is not only fluid, never leaving our thoughts time to blossom in its perpetual race forward; it's also impermeable, in that it forbids any exchange of wealth between our minds and its matter.

At the beginning of the week, as I was finally preparing to launch into my study of Titian Vecellio and Charles V, my upstairs neighbors, Uwe and Inge Drescher (which we might loosely

translate into French as Guy and Luce Perreire), came knocking
at my door. They were going to leave for vacation the next day,
and they were wondering if I might be willing to look after their
plants in their absence. You can imagine my consternation. They
suggested I come up for coffee later that same day so they could go
over my tasks and give me the necessary particulars. After lunch,
I climbed the stairs to their apartment. Receiving me somewhat
coldly, they silently offered me a seat at their round dining-room
table, not yet cleared, still laden with dirty plates and a blue enamel
casserole full of half-desiccated cold pasta, inextricably tangled
and glued together. Uwe Drescher (Guy) disappeared for a moment, then returned from the kitchen with a pot of boiling water.
Having doled out two spoonfuls of instant coffee for each of us, he
cautiously filled the cups with boiling water and began to lay out
my plant-watching duties, the volume and frequency of the watering, the technique to be applied, the sort of water to be used;
just to be sure that everything was quite clear, he reached into his
pocket and pulled out a small sheet of paper, folded in four, which
he'd drawn up for my use. He casually slid it across the table in
my direction, and I looked it over distractedly, drumming my fingers on the tabletop. It was a plant-by-plant summary of my tasks,
briefly recapitulating the various watering frequencies and any
special requirements I should be aware of. I wordlessly folded the
sheet and put it away in my pocket. Uwe gave me a pleased smile,
took a sip of coffee, and invited me on a tour of the apartment
to see the plants. Slowly we strolled from one room to the next,
Uwe leading the way, very tall and bespectacled, smiling a grati-

fied smile, distinguished and enigmatic, one hand rustling in his trouser pocket, jingling his change (maybe he was going to give me a little something), and Inge beside me in her clingy little dress, very much the mistress of the house, occasionally pausing before a plant for an informal introduction, notifying the plant in German that I would be looking after it for the summer (I'm always a little surprised to meet a plant that speaks German). Reserved as I am, I scarcely said hello, limiting myself to a simple, discreet half-blink in the plant's direction, my cup of coffee in my hand. We entered Uwe's study, a study in every way comparable to my own one floor below, with the same French doors and the same little balcony, onto which Uwe suggested the three of us venture for a moment. It was a bit cool outside, and a light wind was blowing. I stood with my elbows on the railing, my mind elsewhere. Paying virtually no attention now to Uwe's botanical explanations (head down, I was absentmindedly dropping pebbles on the passers-by in the street), I cast only a polite little glance at the fertile, dark soil he was showing me, running his marveling finger the length of the planter, in which, here and there, one could indeed make out several little daisy tots. Standing next to me, Uwe pointed an experienced, loving finger toward each newborn seedling, and I nodded slowly and sadly, vaguely hunched over the soil. We returned to his study, and, as my gaze lingered on the various files piled on his desk next to his computer and printer, Uwe drew my attention to an old rubber tree on the mantelpiece, with lovely, dense, dark leaves, indifferent and taciturn as an old Chinaman, which only half listened in as Uwe informed me of its needs, above all that it preferred a light misting to a copious dowsing (which is entirely understandable on the part of an old Chinaman). On the floor sat a begonia with a fragile stalk, and now it was Inge, taking over for her husband, who asked me to be so kind as to perform a very gentle resurfacing of its topsoil in two weeks or so, which means simply scraping away the old dirt around the stalk and replacing it with a good light mixture, of which I would find a five-liter bag in the hall closet, but I wasn't to worry, it was all written down on the sheet. Furthermore, Inge would be grateful, she added, familiarly taking my arm to lead me out of the room, if, during the resurfacing, I wouldn't mind poking a bamboo chopstick into the pot a few times, so as to make aeration holes in the peat. Yes, of course, I said, aeration holes in the peat (she could count on me), and she gave my forearm a little squeeze of anticipatory gratitude, discreet but ardent. In the front hallway, as the Dreschers stood waiting side by side at their bedroom door, I lingered dreamily before a small painting hung on the wall, briefly studying it, my coffee cup in my hand, wondering what it was supposed to depict (an aularch, shall we say). Rejoining the Dreschers, I walked ahead of them into the bedroom, continuing onward for a few indecisive steps, distractedly pushing aside the limp branch of a plumbago that drooped from a macrame hanger, then finally coming to a halt in the middle of the room, glancing toward the Dreschers' large double bed. I went and sat down. Sitting on the Dreschers' bed, I slowly stirred the contents of my cup, withdrew the little spoon, and sucked it dry. With a perfectly serene gaze I made a slow circular sweep of the room, and for a moment I looked up to consider the plumbago. I took a small sip of coffee and set the cup back onto its saucer. You know, life. The Dreschers stood before me, slightly uncomfortable to be with me here in their bedroom; finally they sat down as well, Uwe on the edge of a wooden table, affecting a casual attitude, his right hand still in his trouser pocket, his carefree left hand caressing a gardenia leaf with controlled agitation, and Inge beside me on the bed, slightly stiff, discreetly tugging at the hem of her dress to protect her upper thighs from my supposed Jesuitical prurience, or at least to shield them from the several prudishly covetous glances I must surely be casting their way, then finally standing up to show me her most precious possession, a fern, a magnificent fern, it's true, moist and spreading, and as she fingered it lovingly she confessed that it was fragile and delicate, and that it would be best to prepare it gently for my coming, lest it take fright when I reappeared all alone to give it a sprinkle. I stood up and forced myself to caress a few fern leaves as well, using the knobby thing on my key-ring. The Dreschers appreciated that, I think. In the entryway, as I was leaving, they handed me a copy of their key.

The first time I went up to the Dreschers' after they'd left for vacation (to water and have a little chat with their plants, as requested) was that day in late July when I stopped watching television. After dinner, I'd gone into the living room and stretched out on the couch with my newspaper, very determined not to turn on the TV. With the dark set before me, I calmly read the paper in the dimly-lit living room, secluded in a little pool of slanting light from the halogen reading lamp I'd turned on beside me (the warm, golden glow skimmed neatly over the top of my head, ringing my bald pate with a most attractive duckling-like down). It was obviously not for the purpose of pointless self-mortification that I'd sat down directly facing the set; rather, I wanted to test my capacity for resistance in the very presence of the object of temptation, so that I could turn on the TV at any moment if it turned out my will wasn't up to the challenge. In times past, I frequently didn't watch television when I found myself alone in the evening, and simply did something else, reading or listening to music for example, to remain in the realm of decency; this evening, though, television had taken on a disproportionate importance for me simply because I'd made the decision to stop watching it, and, although it pained me to admit it, television now completely occupied my thoughts. But I pretended otherwise. I opened my newspaper, and, with a nice little cushion nestled behind my nape, quietly read the TV listings in front of the silent set.

I hadn't once thought of the Dreschers' plants since their departure, now some three weeks past (they'd set off at more or less the same time as the Tour de France), and it was only that evening, as I lolled in the living room in my pajamas before going to bed, that I happened onto their list of instructions. I reread it pensively and, troubled by a certain remorse, concerned in spite of myself for the welfare of the plants they'd left in my care, I decided to go up and pay them a little post-prandial visit. Climbing the dark stairs to the Dreschers' in my pajamas (the lights in the stairway weren't working), I met a rather odd character coming downstairs on tiptoe, carrying

JEAN-PHILIPPE TOUSSAINT

a white leather gym bag that looked unusually heavy. In the darkness, I thought I glimpsed several stereo components and some silverware hastily stuffed inside it. I stopped in the middle of the flight, my hand on the banister, and watched him continue down the stairs. He picked up his pace. I stood motionless, my watering can in my hand (I'd brought my own, a big galvanized-tin one). The stranger furtively looked over his shoulder and gave me a quick glance before disappearing. Our relationship ended there (he could be in prison by now for all I know). Arriving on the third-floor landing, I bent over the lock and turned the key, cautiously pushing open the Dreschers' door. I was feeling a little uneasy. I fumbled for the light switch in the entryway and took a few steps down the hall. There wasn't a sound to be heard in the Dreschers' apartment. I noiselessly entered Uwe's study, silent and deserted in the semi-darkness. There was no one in the room, notwithstanding the rubber tree, ever faithful to itself on the mantelpiece, mute, aged, smooth, Chinese. Its tranquillity soothed me, and I sat down on Uwe's desk chair to collect myself. I stood up, my watering can in my hand, opened the French doors, and went out onto the balcony for a breath of night air. But no sooner had I set foot on the balcony than I threw myself back against the wall and froze. Do you know what was happening? Glancing down into the street below, I'd caught sight of the evil-doer I'd met on the stairway a few moments before, now engaged in a hushed discussion with one of his accomplices (a woman, or a man in a wig), who was helping him stow the gym bag in the back of a stolen van. I was witness to a burglary, just my luck. I stood there motionless on the balcony in my pajamas, holding my breath, my watering can in my hand. The streets of this residential neighborhood were soundless at that hour; listening closely, I managed, thanks to my good knowledge of German, of German language and culture I might even say (I'd undertaken a serious study of German since my move to Berlin), to make out a few snatches of their conversation. "What sort of guy?" the woman was asking. "He was bald," said the other one, "a bald guy in pajamas." He glanced up toward the building. "With a watering can," he added. "A bald guy in pajamas with a watering can," the woman said, and she began to laugh uncontrollably, a bald man in pajamas with a watering can on the stairway, it was just too hilarious. "And he thought you were stealing something," she managed to add before succumbing to another fit of laughter. She was laughing so hard that she nearly collapsed onto the sidewalk, but at the last moment she clutched at the man's arm and saved herself. "Yeah, you should have seen the look on his face," he said, and began to laugh with her. Everyone in the street was laughing now—it felt like another country. Standing on the balcony in my pajamas, my watering can in my hand, even I found myself caught up in the general merriment, and I repressed an irritated little smile.

A few minutes later I was in the Dreschers' kitchen, wrapped in a dressing-gown (I'd hastily thrown a dressing-gown over my pajamas, a large plaid one of Uwe's, with wide, flared, satin-stitch embroidered sleeves), filling my watering can from the faucet, forearms bared, trying not to dampen my feet. I turned off the tap, let the last droplets dribble into the can, as you do after a pee—the Dreschers' faucet was fitted with one of those limp rubber foreskins whose flexibility lets the housewife aim the stream wherever she wants it—and then, having completed this operation, straining to hoist my tin watering can, now heavy with several liters of water, I set out into the apartment clutching the can in my right hand like a suitcase. Reaching the entryway, I delved into my pocket for the list the Dreschers had left me and reread it distractedly. Good Lord, how am I supposed to wade through all this botanical German? And where do I begin? Here's the complete text of the list, which might help to illustrate my perplexity. Kitchen windowsill: Parsley and basil seedlings. Everyday (insofar as possible). Kitchen: Small pot of thyme. Twice a week. Entryway: Yucca. Once a week. Study: Ficus elastica (Misting is welcome. Little care required). Begonia (Never dampen the leaves. No misting. Resurfacing essential, every two weeks: change the soil, turn it over all around the root). Balcony: Daisy seedlings. Every day (insofar as possible). Bedroom: Gardenia (Never dampen the leaves. Polishing is welcome. Water twice a week). Fern (Considerable care required: twice a day if very hot; once a day if not. No polishing). Hibiscus (Little care required). Plumbago (Twice a week). This was followed by two blank lines, and then an intimidating little nota-bene in a feminine hand, large, enthusiastic, not unpiquant. N.B. Plants love music! OK. I folded the sheet, slipped it pensively into the breast pocket of my pajamas. What on earth was I going to sing for them?

Arriving in Uwe's study, I was pleased to find the rubber plant still on the mantelpiece. I should say that I'd taken a shine to that silent plant, with its large oval green leaves, like ears, their surface so smooth that they might have been painted with lacquer. I liked the impassive melancholy exuded by that rubber plant, its Sphinx-like quality, its calm, its detachment, what you might call its fundamental indifference to its environment. If it could talk, it would yawn: such would be its revelation, its only comment on the world around it. Not even a reproach. I advanced into the room, the watering can in my hand, paying no further attention to the rubber plant. It had earned my esteem. I imagine it was grateful for my discretion. I merely gave it a thoughtful glance as I entered, just from the corner of my eye, and then I quickly looked away. I've always liked these modest friendships, all tact and quiet reserve, all silence and inexcitability. Which is exactly how this was: it was almost as if I weren't there at all. I blotted my forehead. All this trouble I was going to. I squatted down next to the watering can, pushing my dressing-gown sleeve up to the elbow, dipped in my hands, and stood up to let the water drizzle from the improvised sprinkler of my fingers, showering the leaves with a thousand whirling droplets. I repeated this operation two or three times, bending over the watering can and wiggling my fingers in the water for a moment (out of pure lasciviousness, pure lasciviousness), before withdrawing them to bless the rubber plant from a distance, one last time, with a quick, careless aspersion.

Sitting in the Dreschers' bedroom, my chores at an end, I granted myself a short break on the bed with the watering can at my feet (the Dreschers' bed had become my general headquarters for this operation). The room sat silent and orderly around me, the Dreschers having taken care to leave nothing lying around on the chairs when they left for vacation. Behind the door, Inge's négligée hung on a nail, light and filmy, ideal for a brutal crumpling in a clenched hand; at its feet sat a pair of slippers, not so sexy, pale blue, more inhibited. The few green plants in this room appeared to have been abandoned since the beginning of summer, as if left to their own devices, their leaves withered, yellowed, dusty, crazed in spots. The fern was a pitiful sight, limp in its pot, drooping down over the rim in a sad parody of a weeping willow, its leaves drained, its epidermis wrinkled. It must have suffered more in the heat than the others. I took out the Dreschers' list to reread what was said of this fern. Considerable care required (ah yes, considerable care, just what I was saying), Twice a day, if very hot; if not, once a day. In other words, I'd fallen far short of the mark. Nevertheless, I began to fear, without moving from my spot (this was all pure conjecture, most pleasant to indulge in on the Dreschers' bed), that, if I watered the fern too copiously now, it might wilt good and proper. In the end, hoping to spare it too great a thermic jolt, I went into the kitchen and filled an old basin with warm water; then, back in the bedroom, removing the pot from its shelf, I set it to soak for the night so that the plant might return to life at its own speed, by a slow, progressive infiltration of the moisture, by osmosis and capillarity, and so recover the vigor and splendor of times past. I'd gone and sat down on the Dreschers' bed again, and now I was gazing dubiously at the fern marinating in its lukewarm bath. To think: here I was in Berlin, after ten o'clock in the evening, sitting in my pajamas on the upstairs neighbors' bed worrying about a fern. Before heading downstairs, I took off Uwe's dressing gown and hung it next to Inge's négligée behind the door (the dressing gown had a bit of an odor to it, in spite of everything; I then sniffed at Inge's négligée and there it was again, that same little odor you always find on other people's nightclothes, warm and slightly sour). I turned out the light and stood in the doorway for a moment, looking at the fern in its basin in the dark, a handful of leaves strewn languidly over the carpet. I gently closed the bedroom door and left the Dreschers' apartment, and I started down the stairs, my watering can in my hand, enjoying the sense of a job well done.

Arriving home, I went and turned off the little halogen lamp I'd left on in the living room and, feeling my way through the darkness, I walked toward the window. It was pitch dark outside, and I could just make out the straight, even line of the nearby roofs in the night. A few televisions were still on here and there in the windows of the buildings across the street, bathing the living rooms in a sort of milky glow. Every ten seconds or so, in two quick steps, with each change of scene in the program being screened, this glow disappeared and was replaced by another cone of light, which immediately flooded the available space. I watched the lights shifting and changing together, or, if not together, at least in successive, synchronous bursts, presumably corresponding to the various shows they were watching in the various apartments before me, and this vision gave me that same painful sense of multiplicity and uniformity as the sight of thousands of flashbulbs going off in a stadium during an important sporting event. I went on looking outside, standing there in my pajamas at the window, and I didn't know if I should interpret what then happened as a sign from destiny, a small gesture of personal encouragement that the heavens had decided to offer me as a reward for abandoning the secular joys of television, but, at that very moment, in one of the windows of the tall modern apartment building directly across the way, on the fourth floor to be precise, a young woman appeared in her apartment, stark naked. This envoy from the heavens (I recognized her immediately, she was a student I'd already seen two or three times around the neighborhood) was entirely nude, and delectable in every way. She made me think of some creature painted by Cranach, Venus or Lucretia, that same svelte form, fragile, almost helicoidal, breasts as venial as minor sins and next to no hair on her pubis, just a frail blonde lock, a bit tousled and unkempt at the most intimate spot. Apparently she was looking for her pajamas, or what took the place of pajamas, a sailor's t-shirt with blue and white horizontal stripes, which at last she found and lazily pulled on before picking up a bottle of mineral water from a table and slowly walking away from the window, her bottom bare under her striped t-shirt, giving me plenty of time to observe the undulating progression of what was then my most beloved element of her decor, framed in the glowing screen of that window in the night, until at last she disappeared and turned off the light. The heavens had signed off for the evening.

The next morning I got up at quarter to seven and ate breakfast alone in my Berlin apartment's large dining room. I pensively ate a soft-boiled egg in the dusky, rose-tinged morning light, vaguely listening to the seven o'clock news on the radio, my face drowsy but my mind already fully active, mentally erecting various arabesques, very free, very agreeable to follow, corresponding to the many different directions my monograph might take (I've always liked these informal working breakfasts with myself). Then, my breakfast at an end, as I passed through the chiaroscuro of the apartment to make my way toward the study, I caught a fleeting glimpse of myself in the entryway mirror, and I found this image of me to be rather a true one, that tall, hunched form in the half-lit hallway, a cup of coffee in one hand, advancing at dawn toward the study and its thousand untarnished promises of good work to come. My mind still keenly focused, I switched on the computer, which bade me welcome, sputtering like a coffee maker. I pensively opened the hard drive icon with a quick click of the mouse. Wasting no time, from among the dozen or so vaguely bluish folders that appeared before me in the electronic window I'd opened, I selected the file titled *The Paintbrush* and opened it with two more quick strokes of my finger over the mouse's clitoris, expertly teasing its little ductile zone. Almost without transition, a vast expanse appeared before me on the screen, luminous and grayish. I raised my head, my gaze fixed, and began to think. I took a pensive sip of coffee and set the cup down onto its saucer. But nothing came.

For three weeks now I'd been trying in vain to get down to work. The fact is that I'd run up against a very thorny little question in the first moments of my labor, the first time I'd strode into my study in the glorious, filtered dawn light and switched on the computer, and, rather than resolve that question at once, with the instinctive self-assurance that marks all decisions made in the heat of a project's beginnings, I'd chosen to weigh and consider it at length from various different points of view, and so soon found myself thoroughly paralyzed, unable to begin my work, let alone continue it. I'd stood up and opened the French doors, I'd gone out onto the balcony to pursue my meditation, staring down into the street. The troublesome little question thus occupying my thoughts was simply what to call the painter I would be talking about, what name to give him, Titian, *le Titien*, Vecelli, Vecellio, Tiziano Vecellio, Titian Vecelli, Titian Vecellio? To be sure, such a question might seem trivial compared to the enormous task I'd set out to tackle, my vast analysis of the relations between political power and the arts in sixteenth-century Italy, but it also seemed to me, not to get too abstruse about it, that if one wanted to write it was perhaps not entirely frivolous to consider the question of naming with some care. Let me briefly summarize the scope of the question as it appeared to me that first morning. In the thirty-odd books and monographs I'd read or skimmed in the course of my research, I'd observed the authors who'd written on Titian Vecelli, or Vecellio (even his surname has never been historically established with certainty, and varies slightly from one source to the next, sometimes Vecelli, with an "I," sometimes Vecellio, with an "o") never quite agreed on his name. Broadly speaking, I'd found two distinct approaches to this question: some authors, the majority, among them Victor Basch and Jean Babelon, simply called him Titian, while others, whose ranks included for example Alfred de

Musset and some French translators of Erwin Panofsky, preferred to append a little definite article before his first name and refer to him as *le Titien*, in the quaint manner of the French country-folk.

I stood up from my desk and sat down some distance away in my study to think. My jacket was still draped over the back of the chair, and I looked pensively at the desk as if I could see myself sitting there working (but this was sheer illusion, I hadn't worked for a long time). I could see the corners of the desk's thick, transparent plate of glass sticking out on either side of my jacket. The computer was still on, purring in the center of the desk, the screen scintillating imperceptibly when you looked at it, the printer to its right in standby mode, the green light glowing, a hundred-some white sheets in the tray, and to its left various books and colored folders containing the bulk of my documentation. Legs crossed, I sat in my armchair, one of those black canvas director's chairs with right-angled metal arms, identical to the one in the dining room, and more or less comparable to two others we had in the living room. The French door in my study stood half open, and I could see a few birds pecking on the balcony before me. I sat motionless in my armchair, pensive, watching the tiny white clouds drift lazily through the Berlin sky. Almost everything about my position at that moment recalled Charles V, I thought, the weary Charles V of the Munich Alte Pinakothek, his face pale and pathetic, a glove in his hand, sitting there in his monastic chair as if for all eternity. I of course had no glove in my hand, but, sitting there motionless in my director's chair, my face grave, no gleam in my eye, one hand carelessly poised on an arm of the chair, I must have exuded the same sense of quiet, worried serenity one sees in the Emperor as Titian caught him in Augsburg, sitting before a rich background of gilded Moroccan leather, his body weary and dignified, his face pale like mine, the same disquiet in his gaze. What were we thinking about? What were we so serenely afraid of?

Sitting in my study, I looked at the glowing computer before me and mused that my desire to see this monograph through might simply have abandoned me. Three or four years had now passed since the idea had first come to me, in a rush of enthusiasm and something like exaltation, as I stood in the Dahlem Museum before a portrait of Charles V by Amberger, and since that day the project had only ripened in my mind. The first time I'd mentioned it aloud was to my parents, during a later visit to Brussels; then I'd spoken of it to Delon, and, enthusiastically, to my colleagues D. and T. I'd even laid out the general scope of my study in a little essay that I later used for my grant application (in which I'd further clarified and refined it, as well as Germanizing it a bit). I'd often had occasion to speak of my project since coming to Berlin as well, and whenever, in some public place—a reception, a vernissage—some attractive young Teuton came along and asked in her charmingly hesitant and cautious French what I was doing here, I always mentioned my grant, my *bourse* (an arcane little joke that I savored in secret, knowing that with that word I was evoking both my funding and my balls), and began to describe my idea in its most alluring light, underscoring all that was exciting and new about it, everything innovative and ground-breaking. Recently I'd even caught myself bringing up my project on my own initiative, at parties or dinners at home, sometimes with such enthusiasm that I had to wonder if in the end it wasn't myself I was trying to convince of its interest, and not my unfortunate audience. Once again, it seemed, I was discovering the truth of the rule, a rule I'd never explicitly formulated to myself, but whose veracity I'd quite often sensed in a vague sort of way, which was that the chances of seeing an idea through to completion are inversely proportional to the time you've spent talking about it beforehand. For the simple reason, it seemed to me, that if you've already extracted all the pleasure from the potential joys of a project before you've begun it, there remain, by the time you get down to it, only the miseries of the act of creation, its burdens, its labors.

Sitting with my legs crossed in my director's chair, I then mused that this simple but powerful little displacement of pleasure in the pursuit of most human endeavors might have catastrophic consequences where artistic creation was concerned. Then, following the current of my thoughts, I quite naturally came to ask myself what role television might have played in the fact that people nowadays— entrepreneurs, artists, politicians—seemed to devote more time and energy to discussing their actions than to the actions themselves. Clearly television was not unimplicated in this very general sort of decline; but it then occurred to me that TV could be made still more injurious to artistic creation, for instance by airing programs on which artists would be invited to come and discuss their upcoming projects. Disdaining the works they've completed in order to focus on the ones they plan to create in the future, artists—the most fashionable ones to begin with, but the same principle could easily be expanded to cover all of them—would thus find in television an opportunity to exhaust all their latest project's pleasures in advance, making its actual execution, and in the end artistic creation itself, perfectly unnecessary. And there's no doubt that these artists could speak far more compellingly and convincingly of projects for which they haven't yet raised a finger, and for which their energy and enthusiasm remain undiminished, than of some work they'd just completed, something fragile and delicate and cherished that they would defend with their dying breath, and which they'd never be able to talk about with the requisite casual wit.

I turned off my computer, whose continuous faint electric hum seemed to give way to a sudden sigh of relief, as if the machine were gently decompressing. I stood at my desk for a moment and looked out the window. It was a beautiful day, and I decided to go out for some fresh air. I was wearing canvas trousers and a summery white shirt, my bare feet shod in light deck shoes with a false decorative lace running along the rim of the upper, entering and exiting the leather through a series of lateral holes. Reaching the Arnheimplatz, not far from my apartment, I began to follow a low box hedge that bordered a deserted parking lot. A few businesses stood across the asphalt, most of them closed in July, a laundry, a bicycle shop, and a hair salon. A bit further on, in an open space closed off by a little balustrade of stucco columns, the grounds of a lawn-ornament shop displayed rows of imitation ancient statues, plaster shepherds and Praxiteles adrift in the sparse grass, rotund little fountains, ultrakitsch ersatz bas-reliefs. I entered a little newsstand I liked and lingered for a moment among the shelves. Distractedly I took a newspaper from a stand and made for the front counter, where I laid it down by the cash register. "I'd like some towels as well," I said in my best German accent. "Excuse me?" said the woman behind the counter. "Towels," I said. I stood there in front of her and smiled politely, in the position of slight inferiority that always comes with an imperfect knowledge of the local language. "Maybe you don't sell towels?" I said, with the tinge of irony that is sometimes my way. "No," she said. "And what are those?" I said, affably (not meaning to humiliate her), pointing at the many packets of Kleenex lined up behind the counter. "Those are Kleenex," she said. "Well, I'll take one of those instead, then," I said. "Kleenex. How much do I owe you?" I continued in my best German accent. She must have taken me for a tourist, in my straw hat. "Excuse me?" she said. With both hands, she gestured me to wait for a moment, quickly scrawled "two marks thirty five" on a piece of paper, and held it up before my eyes with an expression of exasperated angelic patience. I paid and left the store. (Taschentuch: Kleenex, Handtuch: towel, such a fussy language).

It took me several tries to cross the street, my newspaper in my hand and my jacket draped over my arm (I'd taken it off, because it was really very warm). On my first try, I only made it one step beyond the narrow ribbon of cinder track that formed the bike path before I was forced to step back by an approaching car whose driver, visibly as furious as he was in the right, probably could have done nothing more than honk to avoid killing me. On my second try, with three carefully timed gazelle-like bounds, I managed to reach the concrete median between the two fast lanes of the urban highway that runs in a complex tangle of thoroughfares through northern Berlin, where the inner ring road—offering access to both Tegel airport to the north and the Steglitz area and Zehlendorf to the south—intersects with the highways that lead toward the west of the country, Frankfurt or Cologne, and in the other direction eastward toward Tegel, Dresden, and even, I thought, Poland. "If I were you, I'd ask someone else a little further on," I advised, pointing toward the area of the Funkturm, bent double beside the passenger window of a little sky-blue car made of corrugated tin that had just stopped beside me on the shoulder, the car's two occupants leaning in my direction and looking at me mystified (maybe they didn't understand German). I watched the little car speed off toward Poland and its sad fate as I waited for yet another wave of cars to go by. The cars always came in these successive salvos, with only the briefest of respites between one blaring surge and the next, a little hiatus that a pedestrian such as I might have been able to put to good use were it not for the almost inevitable materialization of one last car poking along between the two principal waves, preventing my crossing again and again, most recently for example a slow-moving police car, its siren silent, its two occupants glancing at me with an inquisitive eye, mentally evaluating how great a threat to the public order might be posed by a guy like me standing in the middle of a highway in a straw hat. Finally the way was clear, and I could cross. I stepped over the little parapet that secured the guardrail, and from there it was only a short walk along a weedy little hedge to the main entrance of Halensee Park.

On Halensee Park's clipped green lawns, gently sloping down to the lake, three or four hundred people lay outstretched or sat cross-legged, most of them naked, sunbathing, a handkerchief over their heads, or flat on their stomachs, reading a newspaper, or straddling multicolored canvas camp-stools and eating tomatoes, or lounging in trans-Atlantic chairs, ice-chests at their sides. A crowd of bicycles was scattered over the hillside, each with its owner lying on his back in the grass, his hands behind his nape, his member lolling to one side, or flat on his stomach, a red cap on his head, slowly turning the pages of a book open before him. Many more people were swimming in the lake, or chatting at the water's edge, like at the steambath, towels around their waists, a wet-haired bather paddling along at their feet; still others were strolling or running, keeping their distance from the water, where children splashed and flung inflatable life-rings at each other. Everywhere people were sitting on the grass, dazed by the heat, in clusters or alone, some of them fully dressed or simply bare-chested, grave young Turks in heavy jackets and leather pants as if holding council around a non-existent fire, surrounded by empty beer cans lying crushed in the grass, now and then looking around as they spoke for a peek at the naked bodies of the nearby young women, the white bottoms glistening with suntan lotion offered up to the blazing fire of the sun and of their sunglass-shaded eyes. Dogs went racing over the lawns, their snouts skimming the ground as they followed some trail or other, sniffing at any interesting recent droppings they might come across, or crushed tin cans, or the exposed sexual organs of some aged person lying supine, who immediately sat up with a cry of disgust, chased away the dog with a rolled-up newspaper, and stood to continue the torrent of invectives. Several others watched this scene in silence, standing or simply half-sitting up on their rumps, smiling at their immediate neighbors, offering their various comments. Propped up on one elbow in the shade, on a gentler slope of the hill, a punk of at least thirty-five, her hair cut in a Mohawk and her black leather jacket battered and grimy, stared with disgust over her fellow citizens, a piece of straw between her lips. Before her, near a little path winding along the lakeside in the shade of the tall trees, mommies pushed their babies in strollers, followed by dogs and children's bicycles, by daddies with gaily laughing children on their shoulders, while a breathless and helmeted cyclist zigzagged along, honking, clearing a path for himself through the crowd, sometimes braking abruptly on encountering an unforeseen obstacle, a small child running ever further behind an escaping ball, the wheelchair of some improvident invalid, screeching to a halt and then starting off again with great thrusts of the pedals, responding to the insults in his wake with one single finger raised heavenward.

I'd sat down on the grass in a slightly less crowded spot, a few meters away from a young Asian in a white shirt, quiet as an icon, a spiral-bound notebook in her hand, her black hair pulled back and held by a white ribbon. Unmoving, her pen in her hand, she seemed to be drinking in the sweetness of the surrounding nature, pensively gazing at the trees and the little birds posed on the fringe of the branches as if preparing to compose an elegiacal poem, her legs stretching out timid and parallel from under a blue pleated skirt. Before us, in the shade of a tall oak tree, a couple was playing Ping-Pong on a stone table with a permanent metal net. They weren't wearing a stitch of clothing apart from their socks and shoes, neither shirts nor warm-up suits, which didn't stop them from playing a truly merciless game, clenching their paddles, terrycloth sweat bands around their wrists, conceding each point only after an exceptionally fierce contest, leaping backward to return the ball with a desperate flailing blow, their whiplashed torsos arched, then throwing themselves forward for a mighty spike at the slightest opening, hurtling toward the table and accompanying their swats with great grunts of effort and pleasure. The young woman was serving, sweating and focused, not a woman I'd care to take on in any sporting context, tan and muscular down to the interior adductors of her thighs, imparting a vicious curve to the ball with a sweeping thrust of the forearm, then leaping into the air for a spike, clenching a raised fist next to her resolute face whenever she scored a point. Now and then she had to go and pick up a ball that had fallen into the grass, and I soberly inclined my head to one side, the better to see her little slitted rut as she leaned forward (on the whole, I rather enjoyed this little match).

Laying my jacket and newspaper on the grass beside me, I began to undo the buttons of my white cotton shirt, one by one, to let it gape open over my breast. Given the heat, I thought I could justify bending the rules of urban vestimentary convention a little. Cross-legged on the grass, my shirt hanging open but my socks and hat still in place, I began lazily reading my newspaper. I read a not particularly interesting little article on the Tour de France, which had ended the day before; then, slowly unfolding the large rustling pages before me, I looked through the culture section, read a concert review, and went on to the TV listings. For some time, I'd noticed, the space set aside for the TV schedule in newspapers had been steadily growing, slowly and insidiously, imperceptibly and relentlessly. Once limited to one single page, generally the last or next-to-last, it had gradually eaten away at its surroundings, and now occupied two pages, or even three or four, or sometimes a whole little fascicule, for that matter. And it seemed entirely reasonable to fear that the day would come, sometime in the not-too-distant future, when the television listings, still confined to the newspaper's last pages for the moment, would finally establish a bridgehead in the area of the front page, then make their way toward the back and unify their forces, leaving only a narrow corridor for the healthy part of the newspaper, one little patch in which the goings-on of the world might be directly discussed.

I closed my newspaper and stretched out bare-chested on the grass. Eyes closed, I felt the sun caressing my face and breast, my thighs burning under the overheated canvas of my pants, and finally

I took off my shoes with my feet, pressing my toes against my heels to pry them away one after the other. My thighs still burning, I undid my belt without sitting up. Still supine, contorting myself on my back, I eased my pants down over my legs, pulled them off, and set them beside me in the grass. For ten minutes or so I stayed as I was, reclining on the grass in my underwear, thinking of nothing, and then I sat up again. I was just too hot. Under the tree, the Ping-Pong game had come to an end; the girl had sat down on the little stone bench near the table to change, taking off her socks to let her feet breathe for a moment in the open air (she had a satisfied look on her face, she must have given her opponent a proper dressing-down). I rose and stood on the lawn, my hat on my head. Apart from my hat, I was wearing only my underwear, rather roomy and pouchless, one of those American styles of underwear that could easily pass for swimming trunks. My outfit thus remained perfectly decent, nothing to worry about there. I took off my underwear. I could feel a few drops of sweat slowly trickling over my temples. I didn't move. I was still as hot as ever; none of this had helped much. A buzzing wasp orbited around my cheekbones and finally disappeared into the distance. I would gladly have smeared a bit of suntan lotion over my shoulders, and also the upper part of my chest, whose flesh was beginning to pinken. Sitting cross-legged beside me, the Japanese woman was now writing in her notebook. She looked up at me, pensive, glancing for a moment at my privates, still thinking, a vague look in her eyes, then began a new sentence. Maybe she was working from nature, who knows. Onto the grass I lay the wisp of light fabric, vaguely compromising to hold in one's hand, that my underwear had become, then took off my hat and carefully set it down with the rest of my things. Entirely naked, I headed off toward the lake.

I made my way down the hillside at a leisurely pace, vaguely uncomfortable, not knowing what sort of manner to adopt, vacillating between a relaxed stride, with great swingings of the arms whose artificiality only emphasized the awkwardness of my advance, and a more dignified posture, more austere, my head held high, which no doubt brought a hard, grim expression to my face (when in fact I was delighted to feel my toes sinking into the warm grass). Now and then I strayed from the most direct path toward the lake, skirting a group of card players gathered around a blanket like a little committee, or veering a meter or two off course to make my way around some fleshy form reclining on an inflatable mattress, or else, my eye watchful and my feet circumspect, conscientiously keeping away from the symbolic limits of a virtual sports-field, marked out at the four corners by sweaters rolled into a ball, where several young men were gaily playing volleyball. I slowed down as I neared the promenade, which one had to cross in full view of the promenaders in order to gain the little pebble beach used by the swimmers. The former were for the most part fully dressed, women in hats and elegant gentlemen out for a leisurely stroll around the lake, a scarf around their necks and newspapers under their arms, exchanging calm, measured words, stopping for a moment and facing each other to consider and put forward some new argument, underscoring its thrust with a smooth, rounded sweep of the hand. I'd seen them coming, I must confess, but it was too late to avoid them now, I couldn't turn around, retreat was impossible, one of them was already addressing me a friendly little wave from a distance. "How are you, my friend?" said Hans Heinrich Mechelius, in dulcet tones, as he drew near.

It was Hans Heinrich Mechelius, poet and diplomat, president of the foundation that had awarded me my grant. Something like sixty years old, I would think, with voluminous backswept silvery hair. That morning he was wearing a black jacket and an elegant turtleneck of fine gray wool, and holding an amber-tipped black cigarette holder. "What a wonderful coincidence, don't you think?" he said as he drew alongside me. He cordially squeezed my hand and very thoughtfully introduced me to the person beside him, the writer Cees Nooteboom, explaining with a hint of contained irony that I was the professor who was writing an essay on Titian in Augsburg. Cees Nooteboom nodded politely, feigning interest in my object of study (Titian, yes, he saw), while Mechelius drew back and looked at the two of us, visibly pleased with this introduction. Mechelius seemed very light of heart that morning; the fine sunny weather seemed to have bolstered his spirits, in contrast to our last meeting, when I'd found him far graver, and very amiably he inquired into my work, our fortuitous encounter apparently striking him as an excellent opportunity for a chat about the progress of my research, and so informally, without fuss you might say, exercising his role as friendly advisor to his grantees. "And how is your work coming along, my friend?" he said, very tactfully stepping forward to remove a bit of grass stuck to my shoulder. Holding the blade between his fingers, he looked at it pensively for a moment, then cast it aside, briskly wiping his fingertips with his thumb as I started to answer (with some reticence, it's true, I've always been rather reticent when it comes to my work). I nevertheless tried to appear as relaxed as I could in the circumstances, standing before him on the promenade, casually folding my arms over my chest as I concluded a brief rundown of the various little difficulties I'd encountered. Cees Nooteboom looked at the ducks in the meantime. He'd cast a few guarded glances my way as I spoke, resolutely facing the lake all the while, and now he was beginning to weary. He took off his jacket and draped it over his forearm (I hope he wasn't thinking of undressing as well). Just then, as we stood on the promenade, Mechelius warning me not to expose myself to the sun for too long at the beginning, a red beach ball landed in the middle of the little group that we formed; never missing a beat, Mechelius immediately picked it up and threw it back with all the skill and easy grace of a minister baptizing a ship, gently tossing it into the arms of the nude, bald grandfather who'd come forward to reclaim his possession. After this feat, Mechelius casually tossed his scarf over his shoulder, took a handkerchief from his pocket, and wiped his hands at some length. "Such a lovely day, isn't it?" he added with a sigh. "Are you planning to stay in Berlin all summer?" "Yes, yes," I said, "for my work." I scratched my thigh. I shifted my weight onto the other leg and rested one fist on my hip, there on the promenade. "Ah yes," he said pensively, "your work," and he puffed at his cigarette holder, taking a little step back to consider me briefly from head to toe. He couldn't get over it. He shook his head with pleasure, by all appearances genuinely delighted to have run into me that morning. "Would you like to come and have lunch with us?" he asked. "At the Flugangst, it's quite close. The terrace is delightful in summertime." I said he was very kind to ask, but I had work to do.

I floated on my back in the lake, some twenty meters from shore, far from the commotion of the water's edge and the roar of the city, which reached my ears only in muffled form. In the distance, almost at the top of the path that wound uphill toward the city center (we were only five minutes from the Kurfürstendamm), I could still make out the minuscule silhouettes of Mechelius and Nooteboom heading off to lunch, still deep in conversation, maybe resuming a discussion that my appearance had interrupted, or maybe they were talking about me (I doubt it). Their jackets in their hands, their strides labored, I saw them struggling up the last few meters of the slope, now and then pressing their hands to their thighs, still addressing each other from a distance, Nooteboom having gained a lead of several meters toward the end, eventually stopping to wait for Mechelius at the top of the hill. In the end, they're really no better off than I am, I thought (which goes to show that working is sometimes better than lunch). I lay on my back in the water and thought about my monograph, my hands limp and relaxed, floating freely beside me under my benevolently curious gaze, my wrists loose, each finger, each phalange basking in the wonderful liquid that bathed me, my legs outstretched and my body suspended, my package emerging slightly from the water like a very simply arranged still life, two plums and a banana, submerged from time to time in a slight swell. You know, work.

I swam back to shore, slowly extending my relaxed arms in the cool, slightly oleaginous water. Sometimes I swam a few meters on my back, smoothly paddling my legs before me, now and then turning my head to avoid an inopportune collision with a drifting tire or a swan (although swans generally have a good eye for this sort of thing). Arriving near shore, I felt a little hesitant to stand up and find myself naked among the other swimmers, and without setting foot on the lake bed I went on swimming almost up to the beach, or crawling rather, in less than a meter of water, my hands in the mud and my shoulders washed by the waves, practically nose to nose with the belly of a little girl towering over me as she played with a ball, naked but for her orange inflatable armbands. Rising to my knees in the mud, I emerged from the water and hurried off to find my things on the lawn. I made a few tai-chi movements on the lawn before I lay down again. A perfectly inoffensive art is tai-chi, often practiced by peaceful old Chinese gentlemen, and of which my mother too, I'd heard, had become a devotee. For my part, I practiced that art as a dilettante, no doubt failing to observe its most elementary rules. Standing at attention, my knees bent, my gaze grave, conscientiously breathing through my nose (I must have looked just like mother), I made a series of protracted gestures in the air, my crumpled shirt and underwear nearby in the grass, my arms tracing sinuous arabesques in the void to represent some fictive battle, solemnly taking a step forward only after a whole ritual cycle of age-old martial movements. My gaze fixed and serious, my fists clenched and my arms dissymmetrical, I thus attacked all manner of old demons, pummeling them in slow motion, throwing them to the ground to finish them off. Finally I sat down cross-legged on the grass and took a deep breath to relax. The Japanese woman, if she really was Japanese (in any event, she didn't look German), had been watching me go through my exercises, slightly surprised, although with a knowing eye, a connoisseur, I imagined. I finished drying my hands on my underwear and picked up my book, the third volume of Musset's complete works.

It was in Babelon's book that I'd first heard of Musset. The one sentence Babelon devotes to the paintbrush story—according to which Charles V bent down before Titian to pick up a brush that had slipped from the painter's grasp—calls it simply "an anecdote that has acquired the status of a symbolic legend since Alfred de Musset got hold of it." He makes no attempt to specify in what text Musset alludes to this anecdote, whether it was an article or a poem or a play, and it was only a few days after I'd first happened onto this sentence (my research was then in its earliest stages) that, by chance, I discovered the title of the text in question. I'd allowed the Centre Pompidou's slow escalators to carry me downstairs to the library (I was still living in Paris at the time), immobile and pensive, arms crossed, peacefully enjoying a superb bird's-eye view of the immense reading room where hundreds of people were quietly devoting themselves to study; reaching the bottom, I'd made for the library's Painting Department and asked the curly-haired, bespectacled young research librarian in charge how I might find a text by Musset in which some mention was made of a meeting between Titian and Emperor Charles V. This young man immediately broke into an eloquent moue to express his complete ignorance (goodness, he hadn't a clue), but he nevertheless began to tap lazily at the keyboard of his computer, doing his duty. Finally, as if by magic, a list of nine Mussets appeared on the screen. "Alfred?" he asked me, looking up. "Excuse me?" I said. I leaned over the counter to glance at the list of nine Mussets displayed on the screen, arranged in the alphabetical order of their various given names (Edouard, Georges, Paul, Raoul), telling myself that only a computer could instantaneously create so many fortuitous little connections, as intriguing as they were devoid of interest. "Alfred?" he repeated, his finger still in mid-air, ready to lunge at the keyboard. "Alfred," I conceded. His finger did its business on the keyboard, and various nomenclatures appeared on the screen, lists of works classified in columns and sub-columns. According to the computer in the Painting Department of the Pompidou Library, Alfred de Musset was the author of some fifteen books, none of them particularly interesting for our purposes, in the opinion of my interlocutor. "No, I'm sorry, I'm not finding anything," he said, and his computer went dark again. "You should go look in Literature," he told me, gesturing toward the far end of the room.

"Musset is Literature," he added, "same as Corneille." "Yes, yes," I said, "but the thing is that I was looking for a work on Titian," I told him. "A work by Musset, right?" he said. "Yes," I said, and I began to explain that it was most likely a text in which Musset freely imagines some meeting between Titian and Charles V. "But Musset isn't Painting," he answered, in an almost exhausted voice. How could he explain? We reflected for a few moments more, the two of us, on our respective sides of the counter. "And I don't suppose Charles V is Painting?" he said—the coup de grâce.

Making my way across the room to the Pompidou Library's Literature Department, I found myself before an ascetic librarian of some fifty years, dressed in a sleeveless pullover and a thick cotton shirt buttoned up to the neck. Laying out the object of my research and the difficulties I'd encountered in locating the Musset text I sought, I asked if he thought himself in a position to help me. He reflected for some time, holding a black pencil which after a moment he placed in his mouth and began to suck (was this a good sign? a bad sign? I feared the worst). It was a good sign. Not only was he prepared to help me, but he was even amenable to a joint consultation of the Pompidou Library's great central computer, taking advantage of this rather unusual opportunity to further his assistant's software training. Rising from his chair, he explained that this was of course an entirely exceptional way of proceeding, and that in principle the role of the Centre's librarians was not to help readers with their research ("No no, of course not!" I said)—by using the Pompidou's computer system, he meant—and then, snatching a tiny key from a drawer, he went and opened a metal cabinet, briefly kneeling down before it, then rising with an ultrathin diskette in his hand. He slowly wiggled it back and forth before my eyes with a sly look, at once mysterious and conspiratorial. "Musset," he told me quietly. "Musset?" I said. "Musset," he confirmed, lowering his eyelids. "All of Musset," he added. "All of Musset!" I cried. I was overdoing it a little (as if I'd never seen a diskette before), but I wanted to make all this worth his while, and for that he seemed grateful, modestly tapping the ultrathin diskette in his hand. Such a child. We approached the Pompidou Library's central computer, and without further ado he slipped Musset into the machine, which immediately began to purr. Now his assistant arrived, a rather portly woman of about sixty in a brown sweater and a gray skirt, with big bifocals and a little gold chain around her neck. She sat down at the computer, carefully arranging her skirt. None too sharp, it seemed. The librarian delicately laid his hand on her shoulder to supervise as she typed the first codes into the computer. "Right, now you type in TIT, Georgette," he said. "TIT?" she said, looking up at him. "TIT," he said. "Titian," he told me. Georgette typed in TIT. The machine began to whir. Georgette waited, her hands parallel over the keyboard. "And now I enter Musset?" she asked, looking up. "No, no, Musset's already there," the librarian answered, his hands shaking, "Musset's already in there." Enter Musset: he turned to me and raised his eyes heavenward. He leaned over the screen for a moment, bringing a fingertip to the glass to wipe away an invisible little flyspeck that was bothering him. Everything was going smoothly, the computer continued to purr, or make coffee, I'm not sure which, giving an occasional sputter. His arms crossed over his chest, like at NASA, never taking his eyes off the columns of numbers displayed on the screen, the librarian leaned over to me and whispered an aside to the effect that we would soon be entering Charlemagne. "Charles V," I said. "Charles V," he said, blushing. He let Georgette enter the emperor into the computer by herself, meanwhile explaining to me that the computer would now compile an exhaustive list of the relevant passages in the Musset corpus, giving us all the necessary references, which we would then have only to print out. Nothing could be simpler. "On a virtual page, of course," he told me. "Of course," I said, what sort of a imbecile do you take me for? A few moments later, five sheets did indeed emerge from the printer, which he inspected after donning his glasses. Running an attentive eye over the five sheets, he gravely handed them to me one after the other, so that I might judge for myself. I took the first sheet and read, "Help Next Last Revise Increment See Num Rem Save All Zoom In Zoom Out Archives End Search 1."

Then, for numbers fans, came the concrete examples ("Ex. 1. Sel. Ex. available 1. 2. for Titian, and 1. 2. 3. 4. for Charles V"). Now things were becoming clearer. In short, if we are to believe the central computer of the Pompidou Library, in all of Musset's writings the word Titian appears twice, first in an 1831 article for the newspaper *Le Temps* and then in *The Confession of a Child of the Century* ("I have seen *le Titien*'s Saint Thomas placing his finger on Christ's wounds, and I have often thought of him"), while Charles

V appears four times, first in an 1831 article for the newspaper *Le Temps*, then three times in *Lorenzaccio*, Act I Scene iii, Act IV Scene iv, and Act V Scene viii. The librarian and I pored over the five sheets, soon joined by Georgette, delighted to have been the source of all this wonderful research, as fruitful as it was erudite. By a simple cross-referencing of the two lists the computer had generated, we soon reached the conclusion that the text Babelon was referring to had to be the 1831 article from *Le Temps*. The goal was within sight. His hands still quivering, the librarian went off and picked up a notebook with a laminated cover, which listed the complete corpus of Musset's writings work by work. He ran his finger slowly down the list, from top to bottom. "Here we are," he said, "articles for the newspaper *Le Temps*, in the *Complete Works*, volume 9, pages 109-110, Paris: Garnier, 1908. 1908, pooh," he said, "unfortunately, I don't believe we own that collection." He put his black pencil into his mouth and began to think. "Microfilms," he said. "Oh, yes, microfilms," Georgette conceded (now it's microfilms, what a glorious day! she thought).

Sitting before the gray screen of a microfilm reader in the Pompidou Library, I watched the 1831 volume of the newspaper *Le Temps* march past before me, now and then halting its progress to read a headline or a bit of an article, or to catch up on the latest sports results. I didn't have a precise page reference for the article I was looking for, and I was beginning to think I'd never find it when, still unwinding the ribbon of light I'd brought to life on the screen, I finally happened onto an article by Musset in the *Revue Fantastique* section, which at least confirmed I was on the right track. After some further meanderings, slowly turning the crank to send the film lurching forward or back (the machine was an antique, probably designed a little before the appearance of the first microfilms), I finally hit on the piece I was looking for, which I skimmed quickly after adjusting the brightness and manually sharpening the image with a touch of the focus button. This was indeed the article published in *Le Temps* in 1831, in which the names Titian and Charles V do indeed appear together, a few lines apart, but nowhere did I find the slightest allusion to the anecdote of the brush that Charles V is said to have picked up in Titian's studio. Pensive, slightly peeved, I removed the microfilm from the reader, relaxing the grip of the plates, and took the box back to the librarian, explaining that I'd found the article ("I knew you would," he said), but that it wasn't the one I was looking for. Deeply skeptical of this claim, the librarian replied that if such was the case, and given that my text couldn't be located in Musset's complete works, then it had to be some sort of uncatalogued rarity, an unpublished text, a bibliophilic curiosity. "Yes, no doubt," I said, and, thanking him, I sadly retraced my steps through the library. In the stacks all around me, readers were studying books they'd pulled from the shelves, quietly turning the pages. Some of them had settled down on the carpeted floor for a more comfortable read, a garment rolled up beside them or a tiny backpack harnessed to their backs; others sat on the heating ducts, absentmindedly paging through a comic book, an anorak on their knees, and beside them a bum in a houndstooth overcoat, apparently weary of the colloquia being held by his fellows up on the ground floor. I entered the stacks and slowly advanced between two walls of books. Now and then I found myself taking a volume from the shelves, leafing through it for a moment, then putting it back in its place. Standing before the Musset collection, which I'd finally located in an aisle given over to nineteenth-century French literature, I bent my head sideways to read the titles on the spines, just out of curiosity, then pulled out the last volume of the Pléiade edition of the complete works. Standing between the shelves, I paged through it briefly, then turned to the end for a look at the table of contents, where I found the very text I'd been looking for, a short story by Musset entitled "Le fils du Titien."

Sitting on the lawn in Halensee Park, I'd now finished rereading Musset's "Le fils du Titien" for the second time in several days, enjoying the succulent little Pléiade volume with its apparatus of invaluable notes, so delightful to gnaw at reflectively, like tiny rabbit bones. I'd made my way through the text with great care, never missing a note reference, flipping conscientiously to the back to discover its contents, and it was only at the end of this reading, cross-legged on the grass in Halensee Park, that I realized, gingerly placing a hand on my shoulder, that I had a sunburn. As for my other problem, the thorny little question of Titian's name, it seemed to me that the editors of the Pléiade edition had done little to settle it, adopting in their notes the partial and rather craven solution of not contradicting Musset in this volume devoted to his works, and so, when they weren't calling him Tiziano Vecellio (page 1129, note 7), regularly referring to Titian as *le Titien*. But it's obvious you can't rely on Musset, I kept telling myself. He even gives Leonardo da Vinci a "le"! Le Vinci! It's right there on page 449 of the story! (Naked in the grass, I seethed with rage at Musset).

I calmly closed my book, set it down beside me in the grass, stretched out on my back, and closed my eyes. I lay motionless, wondering if in the end I wasn't trying to avoid my work as I lay here naked in the park, my feet in the grass, occasionally tickled by the tender blades when a light breeze bent them over my toes. But wasn't this working, I asked myself, this gradual, progressive opening of the mind, this steady sharpening of the senses? And if not, wasn't it at least every bit as gratifying? We know that Michelangelo spent many long hours gazing on the immense blocks of marble he'd had cut from the quarries of Carrara, as if the works to come were already there, imprisoned in the raw mass of stone before him, and his task simply to free them from that rigid casing, gently applying his chisel to push aside anything that might detract from the purity of their eternal forms. And so, still on my back, one hand on my thigh, the other lying free beside me in the grass, I went on pursuing Aristotelian daydreams of my monograph. I've always had remarkable success with this sort of mental labor, it's true, letting the book to come gradually settle in and inhabit me by simply following the thread of my thoughts, doing nothing that might interrupt the flow, and so unchaining a multitude of impressions and reveries, a host of structures and ideas, often incomplete, scattered, unformed, some still gestating, some already fully developed, a wealth of intuitions and insights, of pains and emotions, which I then had only to put into their definitive form.

And, still lying there peacefully in Halensee Park, I reflected that, if your goal is to write, not writing is surely at least as important as writing. But that you should be careful not to overdo it (because that's the one little risk I might be running these days).

Musset sets "Le fils du Titien" in Venice, a few years after Titian's death. He imagines that one of Titian's sons, Pomponio (in fact, Titian had two sons, Orazio, a painter like his father, and the real Pomponio, an incompetent, an ecclesiastic, Babelon can't find words harsh enough for him), painted one single painting in his life, a portrait of his mistress Beatrice; once this canvas was finished, once he'd shown the world what he was capable of and seen his work universally hailed as a masterpiece, he abandoned painting at once and forever. Thus, Musset shows us Pomponio at work on his mistress's portrait, standing at an easel that once belonged to his father, now set up in his bedroom. He carelessly drops a brush to the floor, and his mistress breaks her Crowned Venus pose to pick it up and return it, reminding him of the similar gesture supposedly made by Charles V before his father. Moved by the recollection of this memory, Pomponio goes to a cabinet and takes out the famous brush, preserved by his father like a precious relic, and begins to recall the circumstances of that mythic scene, which he'd witnessed as a young man. As he tells it, the incident took place in 1530, when Charles V came to Bologna for an audience with Pope Paul III (which is of course historically doubtful, if only because Paul III wouldn't become Pope for another four years; rather, the authors of the Pléiade edition suggest, if the brush incident isn't a legend, it must have occurred in Augsburg some twenty years later, when Titian, already an old man, had become the official painter to the court). In Bologna, then, according to Pomponio, Titian was standing high atop a ladder before a very large canvas, lost in his work, when he was surprised by an unexpected visit from the emperor; descending the rungs as quickly as he could, slightly ashamed of the stiffness and slowness visited on him by his advanced age, he apparently knocked his hand against the upright and so dropped the paintbrush. Charles V, Musset writes, then "took several steps forward, slowly bent down, and picked up the brush."

The central idea of my study was to show that what is extraordinary about this anecdote is in the end not so much that the emperor bent down to pick up the brush, but that Titian permitted himself to drop his brush in the emperor's presence. Indeed, no reader can fail to see the lengths Musset goes to in his story to come up with plausible circumstances—excuses, really—for the insolence, outrageousness, and *lèse-majesté* that such a gesture would represent for a Renaissance artist, dropping the instrument of his art in the presence of his most powerful patron; nor should we fail to see how clearly such a gesture might signify that the artist henceforth—and for the first time in the history of art—refused to be treated as a simple tradesman, whose studio one might visit whenever the mood struck, where one might even permit oneself to order such and such a correction, according to one's own whims and fancies. With this gesture, then, the artist was demanding to be treated as a free man, implicitly declaring to the greatest sovereign of his time that his visit, however imperial, was inopportune, and that, having been interrupted in his work, there was no question of going back to his painting until the emperor had withdrawn. Indeed, he would have been perfectly incapable of doing so even if he wanted to, having, as the emperor could plainly see, no brush in his hand. And it's true: how can you paint without a brush? In those days, I mean. Musset's narration is most revealing on this point, for if, to introduce the account of the brush incident, Musset tells us simply that Pomponio dropped his brush by accident, and seems perfectly happy to accept this little contingency as a given, it is on the contrary with a suspicious abundance of pointless justifications that he struggles to make plausible the idea that Titian could have dropped his brush in the emperor's presence, thereby muffling the force of a potentially blameworthy act under a plethora of potential explanations, evoking now Titian's great age, now his surprise at seeing the emperor enter, now the fact that he was forced to lean on the handrail to descend from the ladder he was standing on. And we're supposed to believe that all this would necessarily result in the dropping of the brush? I don't think so.

The reality was quite different. Returning to Augsburg in No-

vember 1550, Titian once again settled into the room that he used
as a studio during his sojourns at the imperial court, a sort of vast,
cold, high-ceilinged gallery, crammed with assistants preparing
his colors and grinding his pigments, mixing spirits, making com-
pounds. A fire burned in the fireplace, and the air was thick with
the odor of turpentine, varnish, and glue. Some of his canvases hung
from the picture rails; others sat on the floor facing the wall, roughly
sketched out over a scumble of red earth or a lead white base, as was
the Master's custom. Sometimes these unfinished canvases could
sit for several weeks before he returned to them, randomly picking
up one or another as he strolled through his studio. Now, dressed in
a simple garment, warm and richly black, with a little crenellated
linen collar emerging from the top, he stood stiffly before his canvas, his gaze intense, almost cruel, a brush poised in his right hand,
his palette in the other, along with a bouquet of four more brushes
fanned out underneath it. His head high, bent very slightly to one
side, very still, the brush in mid-air, he was staring intensely at a
patch of fabric before him, letting his gaze penetrate the texture
and the material, when, at a distant point in his field of vision, he
caught sight of the hallebardiers of the emperor's guard, clatter-
ing down the marble-paved corridor toward the doorway before
him. Not moving a muscle, neither in his eyes nor in his neck, he
completed his scrutiny of the cloth, and then, against all expecta-
tions, without interrupting himself to bow down as the emperor
entered, he shifted his gaze toward the spot on his canvas where
that precious fabric was painted, pale and shimmering, identical
to the cloth he'd just been observing. He was about to add a little

white highlight to emphasize the garment's loft, but now he hesitated, as if the motion inspired by his gaze were not reaching his arm to impart the necessary smoothness, distracted and disturbed as he was by the emperor still silently and slowly approaching, his hands behind his back. The emperor was now only a few meters away; soon, very slightly changing course to make his way around the easel, he would catch his first glimpse of Titian's new work. And it was precisely as the emperor began skirting the easel for a look at Titian's great canvas, well on its way but not yet completed, that Titian changed his mind, deciding to switch to another brush and add a golden highlight rather than a touch of white, and let his brush slip from his grasp. It fell through his fingers and landed at the emperor's feet. Dispensing with the customary greetings and reverences, the two men exchanged a glance of tremendous intensity. The brush lay on the floor at their feet, a tiny gold dot at the tip of its fine, contained flame of hairs. Inclined, its colored point glistening with oil, the brush lay on the marble, and no one in the room made a move. Already the muscles in Titan's back, shoulders, and arms were readying the gesture with which he would bend down and pick up the brush, but Charles V acted first, stooping down to retrieve the brush and return it, thereby implicitly recognizing the precedence of art over political power. Here I might be mistaking my desires for the reality of the scene. That was all; not ten seconds had elapsed from the time of Charles V's appearance in the studio. I was able to time the events precisely one day with my son in our Berlin apartment, myself playing the emperor and my son Titian. He stood before me in the living room, barefoot in his little red pyjamas, his demeanor grave and conscientious, his role not particularly demanding: his only task was to drop one of the four colored felt-tip pens he was holding, on my command. "Go," I said, and he dropped the pen to the floor. Then I slowly bent down, picked up the brush and solemnly returned it. "Alstublieft," I said (let's not forget, the emperor was from Ghent). "Thank you," my son replied (he said these words very simply; the great figures of our world are people like you and me, you know).

Finally I opened one eye, still on my back in Halensee Park, and, as is often the case when you've kept your eyes closed for too long in the sunlight, all the colors of the surrounding nature seemed remarkably clear and brilliant, the green of the grass and the very dense blue of the sky, as if freshly washed by a gleaming, damascened rain shower. I'd now spent more than two hours in Halensee Park, and I was beginning to sense that it wouldn't be much longer before I could go home and start writing. It would be a mistake to suppose that these moments of quiet preparation for writing are irrelevant to the task itself. Indeed, in these moments of profound vulnerability, as our bodies and minds steel themselves for the task to come, our newly-vigilant senses seem to develop a heightened ability to spot all sorts of threats in the world around us, real or imagined, often infinitesimal, sometimes familiar, as likely to arise from an unforeseeable disturbance like the arrival of Charles V as from some less improbable stroke of fate, but in any case, owing to our great emotional and nervous fragility at such times, seeming to rear their heads for the sole purpose of undermining our work, if not the very possibility of sitting down to write. Nevertheless, once one has found the necessary tranquillity of mind, whether through an extraordinary effort of the will or because things have fallen into place almost on their own thanks to a nap or a nice walk, what one must then do, bending all one's forces toward this one single goal, is return to one's desk at once and sit down to work, just as, when you've caught a live butterfly, say, you have to hurry straight home with it, because as long as it's still alive it might take advantage of any little lull in your attention to flee and vanish forever. You have to run home, then, preserving that ephemeral treasure in the sealed shell of your hands, feeling its light, living wings quivering like inspiration within the cage of your curved palms.

Back at home, my mind still keenly focused, my intellect intent on the work at hand, taking care not to let myself be distracted before reaching my desk, I pulled off my jacket in the hallway and headed straight for the study. I sat down and turned on the computer. The beginnings of a sentence had already come to me on my way back from the park. I repeated that sentence to myself mentally, my fingers preparing to type it on the keyboard. "When Musset, taking up in his story . . . " No, that wasn't right, "taking up" wasn't right. I raised my head and looked at the ceiling. "Evoking," maybe? No, "evoking" wasn't right either. On the other hand, "when" sounded pretty good to me. "When" was irreproachable,

I thought. And "Musset," well, it was Musset, there wasn't much I could do about that. "When Musset," I said under my breath. Yes, that wasn't bad. I stood up, walked across the room, opened the balcony door and pensively stepped outside. "When Musset," I repeated quietly. No, there was no denying it, that was a good beginning. I said it a little louder. "When Musset." I rested my elbows on the railing and bellowed a bit: "When Musset! When Musset!" I repeated on the balcony. "When Musset!" "Quiet!" I suddenly heard. "Would you please be quiet!" It was coming from down below me. I leaned over the railing. "Oh, I'm sorry," I said, my head hanging over the void. It was the building's landlord, an elderly gentleman, reading in the garden on a folding chair. He'd set his book down on his knees, and he was looking up at me in surprise, as if something about all this were eluding him. I politely raised my hat in greeting, assuming my hat was still on my head at that moment (if not, my gesture could only have been still more surprising). Just then, in any case, the telephone rang in my apartment, leaving me no choice but to interrupt my work.

Delon (how good it felt to hear Delon's comforting voice beside me in the earpiece), not even taking the time to ask how my work was going, immediately told me how wonderful she was feeling today, and that this morning she'd felt the baby moving in her stomach for the first time. When she was swimming, she told me, the baby was swimming in parallel, she could feel the baby's body moving in her stomach, the baby must have realized that she was in the water as well, and began to swim in her stomach. She fell silent, and I imagined them both swimming in the still Mediterranean waters, deep blue and clear, one above the other, one inside the other, two angels, the big, slow, relaxed one smoothly extending her arms and legs in the limpid water, smiling, happy, laughing her laugh that never stopped when it started up in the water, gradually robbing her of all her strength and at the same time making her want to pee in the water, forcing her to throw back her head and paddle desperately to keep from sinking to the bottom, laughing her wonderful laugh that I so loved in the water, and the other, the little one, not yet born, not even my baby yet, tiny and warm, curled up in the amniotic fluid, suspended in her mother's warm belly as she carefreely swam this way and that in the warm water. Three times already this morning she'd felt the baby move in her stomach, Delon was telling me, she'd never felt so wonderful since the first days of the pregnancy. A few hours ago, she'd even dived to the bottom to look for urchins. And, sitting with the telephone in the living room of my Berlin apartment, I effortlessly conjured up the image of my Delon diving into the clear water this morning to go looking for urchins, this morning or another morning, it doesn't matter, several Delons were now superimposed in my mind, all of them gaily diving through the colored limbo of my memory to look for fresh urchins, her blue mask slightly squeezing her cheekbones, swimming slowly over the surface of the clear water, taking her time, her head half-submerged to inspect the plant life below her. Calmly observing the sea floor from behind the transparent pane of her mask, a twisted fork in her hand and the leather straps of a large wicker basket wrapped around her wrists, she swam more or less in place in the little deserted cove, paddling her long black flippers behind her, leaving a slight foaming wake, and, having no doubt spotted the dark mass of an urchin below her, she suddenly let herself sink straight to the bottom, her outstretched body disappearing completely into the water, her legs vanishing last of all into the waves, elegant and lithe as a naiad, then surfacing again a few seconds later, breathless, her hair hanging over her eyes, a few strands of seaweed clinging to her head and an urchin skewered on the fork, which she examined uncertainly for a moment before dropping it into the basket, her hair falling in two long wet locks over her mask, then diving again, and again and again, until the basket was full, swollen with water and heavy with several dozen lovely fat urchins glistening in the sun, tinged with black and mauve, their spines swaying this way and that. Then, pulling a simple white cotton shirt over her wet swimsuit, she set off for the house, still dripping wet (making a little stop at the fig tree by the side of the road, all the same, an obligatory pause on the way back from the cove, lazily scanning the barren branches before rising up on tiptoe to pluck one or two figs, which she cut open and ate as she drifted homeward, her basket of urchins draped with a beach towel). Back at the house, sitting on a metal chair in the shade of the tall trees in the garden, she began to cut open the urchins with large orange scissors, thrusting the tip of the blade into the body, then slowly running it around the circumference to divide the urchin in two, a plastic basin between her legs for the offal, her hand turning over to dump out the contents with a gesture as quick as it was energetic, carefully emptying the shell, keeping within the urchin's coveted jewel-box only the marvelous edible orange strips that lay fanned out at the bottom of the shell, like fronds of coral in the harmonious form of a star of one magnitude or another, orange giant or red dwarf. With this task behind her (the quickly assembled plate of urchins now on the table, draped in a red-and-white checkered kitchen towel to ward off the flies and the bees), my Delon went and washed herself off with the garden hose, standing in a corner of the garden between the two big tanks of gas that fueled the house, her head thrown back, slowly smoothing her hair in the flowing water. "Well, I'm," I said—but I didn't have the heart to bother her now with my work problems ("Well, I'm not doing so well," I said, "I've got a sunburn.")

"In Berlin?" she said. "You got a sunburn in Berlin?" and she started to laugh. I began to explain, as she went on laughing ("A sunburn in Berlin," she kept repeating, I was just too much), that I'd finally gone out for a walk this morning because I was having some difficulty working. Although, as a matter of fact, just now, just before she called, I explained, I'd just written—I thought for a moment, did a quick calculation—a half-page, or almost a half-page, anyway ("When Musset"). "Where is this sunburn?" she said. She couldn't stop laughing. "On the top of your head?" "On my shoulders," I said. Then, wasting no further time, I asked her for news of the children. "The kid's OK? Not too jealous of the new one?" Because even before she was born, everything seemed to be about the new one these days, I'd noticed (even my work seemed to have been put on the back burner). "No, no, he's wonderful," she said, "he's all tan, if you can imagine that. Do you want me to go get him?" she said, and she was gone before I could answer. "Hello, Daddy," my son said, "how are you?" "I'm fine, kid," I said. My phone conversations with Babelon always began with this little exchange (for the past two or three weeks I'd been calling my son Babelon, I don't know why).

Sitting in the living room of the Berlin apartment, my feet resting on the coffee table next to the telephone, I tipped back in my director's chair and explained to Babelon, who was asking why I didn't come and join them in Italy, that I had work to do, I was writing a book. "What's your book going to be called?" he asked. I told him I didn't know yet, reluctant to disclose the one element of the project that I thought firmly established for the moment, which is to say its title. "What would you call it?" I asked him. "Mimosa," he said. He said this without hesitation, leaving me at a loss for words (maybe he'd been thinking about this in his little bed at night, so he wouldn't be caught short if I ever asked him). "Will you buy me a Ninjet?" he said. "Excuse me?" I said. "Will you buy me a Ninjet?" he said. "A Ninjet? What do you mean?" I said. "The kind you attach to the back of a Power Ranger?" (And me a sixteenth-century specialist.) "An orange Ninjet with two disks that shoot and kill," he said. "All right, we'll see," I said. "Put your mother back on, please." And, while my son went off to find Delon in the garden, no doubt racing through the rooms like the fleet-footed sprinter he was, and while I sat in the living room looking pensively at my bare feet on the telephone table, I wondered if I should tell Delon I'd stopped watching television, at the risk of prematurely announcing a vow I wasn't sure I'd be able to keep.

The Venetian blinds behind me were raised, and the sun poured generously into the living room. A great pool of light stretched out diagonally before me on the wooden floor, glowing, almost alive. Its vague outline shifted slowly with the whims of a light breeze that must have been blowing outside, its boundaries imperceptibly broadening or shrinking, like the lazy to-and-fro of a fan made of shadow and light. Waiting for Delon to come back to the phone, I looked at the smooth, polished parquet in front of me and began to think wistfully of the many games of ice hockey my son and I had played here in our socks, something to see, my Babelon firing his fierce slap shots with the little hockey stick I'd bought for him, drawing it back level with his shoulder to ready his aim and then swinging with all his might at the light little Lego we used as a puck while I stood waiting somewhat awkwardly, knees bent, in the goal (a little table of lacquered black wood that might well have been designed for this very purpose)—or, on the contrary, when it was him defending the goal against my zigzagging improvised Czech charges, a full-face motorcycle helmet on his head, his hands protected by a pair of boxing gloves he'd got for his birthday, when it was me skating freely through the living room in flannel trousers and gray socks, shielding the puck with my stick, my eyes peeled for the slightest opening in my opponent's defense, suddenly slaloming as I approached the goalie to dribble and slip the puck into the back of his nets with one final unstoppable backhand, avoiding a last-ditch body slam from my little four-and-a-half-year-old boy, who launched himself into my calves with the same unstinting ardor as his mother generally displayed when she threw herself into my arms. What a family (sometimes we even went to find Delon in the bedroom so we could show her the last goal in slow-motion replay, languidly miming the action from the beginning with endlessly protracted, ethereal motions of our bodies and sticks).

When Delon finally came back to the phone, I quietly announced that I'd stopped watching television. I calmly awaited her initial reaction, of admiration or surprise. I'd imbued my voice with a certain solemnity to convey this news, and I didn't know if she would congratulate me straight off, finding some tender word to hail my initiative, underscoring my lucidity, for instance, or my courage (although Delon didn't really talk like that, like a politician), or if, simply surprised, she would ask for some further explanation (which I would of course have been reluctant to give her). "Yes, we don't watch much TV here either," she told me.

It was that afternoon that I first had the sense of something lacking, my first pang of withdrawal. I'd stopped watching television at more or less this same hour the day before, after the end of the Tour de France, and it was only now, as I was coming to sit down on the couch in the living room after Delon's call, that I felt this sensation, a sort of impalpable, uncentered pain, which returned to torment me several more times over the course of that day, whenever I spent a few moments in the living room facing the dark television set. It generally manifested itself in brief, violent bursts, waylaying me unexpectedly and momentarily leaving me numb, although, even as I was suffering its torments, I found I could easily tolerate them. For the painful essence of withdrawal does not reside in the present suffering it brings—withdrawal is painless on the level of the immediate moment—but in the prospect of suffering to come, the rich future that one can imagine one's torture enjoying. What is unbearable in withdrawal, then, is the long term, the empty horizon it opens up before you; it's knowing that it will go on, for as long as you can imagine. Whatever you do, from this moment on, you will forever find yourself confronting an adversary before which you stand powerless, for, by its very nature, withdrawal parries all attempts to combat it, infinitely deferring the battle, never giving you a chance to deliver yourself of the tensions you pointlessly accumulate in hopes of overcoming it.

Sitting on the couch in the living room before the dark TV set, I looked at the screen in front of me and wondered what might be on. For one essential characteristic of television, when you're not watching it, is that it makes you think something might happen if you turned it on, something more powerful and more unexpected than what happens to you in your ordinary life. But this is a vain hope, perpetually dashed, because nothing ever happens on television, and the most insignificant incident of our personal lives always touches us more meaningfully than any joyous or catastrophic event we might witness on television. Never does the slightest exchange take place between our minds and television's images, never the slightest projection of ourselves into the world it offers us; never, in the concourse of our hearts, do television's images, so remote from our own thoughts and sensibilities, ever meet up with any real dream, any horror, any nightmare, any joy. They arouse no passion, produce no explosion, but rather, encouraging our somnolence and flattering our phlegmatism, content themselves with simply anesthetizing us.

It was nearly five in the afternoon (I'd just glanced at the clock, absentmindedly), and I was thinking it was too late to try to get back to work now. Sitting on the couch in the living room, I then began to muse on the little problem that had been occupying my mind on and off for what would soon be three weeks, which is to say the name I should give Titian in my monograph, and I tried to console myself for not having made a definitive choice by observing that, paradoxically, what would truly have justified the accusation of avoiding my work and enjoying an easy summer in Berlin would surely have been settling straight down to write without fully considering the question of the artist's name, and that in fact I had every reason to be pleased with myself for having, in a spirit of scholarly scrupulousness and perfectionism, maintained myself for nearly three weeks in a state of perpetual readiness to write, without taking the easy way out and actually doing so.

I leaned over to pick up my newspaper from the coffee table (that was enough work for today, anyway), and I imagine that, if I hadn't then heard a noise in the street (just one isolated noise, not followed by any other) that made me turn my head toward the window and see how filthy the glass was, smudged with the accumulated traces of many urban squalls, shot through here and there with the dusty trails of dried raindrops, it would probably never have occurred to me to wash the windows at that moment. You never know how things are going to turn out, do you? I went into the kitchen and opened the cupboard under the sink, kneeling down to extract a basin and a sponge, as well as the spray bottle of window cleaner, so beloved of my son (for its "tricker," as he said, doubly wrongly, to refer to the lever that operated the pump), which did not prevent him from displaying a particularly itchy forefinger whenever I authorized him, under my imperturbable surveillance, to moisten the windows or coffee table with a spray of that miraculous liquid, which went ssshhht and turned foamy the moment it touched the glass. It's true that this was a fascinating tool, this transparent plastic bulb, full of a limpid, blue solution with a lovely detergent scent. I threw open one of the living room's two French doors, almost two meters high, with a single unbroken pane of glass extending almost to the ceiling, topped moreover by a little transom, and I climbed onto the radiator, the basin at my feet. Standing on the brink of the void, clasping the French door with one hand while the other peppered the glass with the spray from my pistol, I soon realized that, once the first lighthearted spatterings are over, carefree and slightly silly, the window washer's delight, of which Jackson Pollock surely knew a thing or two, the task quickly turns tiresome, for now there's nothing to do but wipe, like some maniacal housewife, firmly pressing your sponge to the glass—or, even better than a sponge, a page from an old newspaper, for, even where windows are concerned, nothing will ever replace the printed page, in my opinion. I thus held in my hand a crumpled sheet of newsprint, and I was wiping the top of the windowpane, standing on the edge of the sill, sometimes leaning perilously into the emptiness to reach some complicated corner and give it a finishing touch with a sponge, when I saw a taxi rolling down the street before me. I stopped wiping for a minute, my sponge in my hand, to watch its approach. Slowly the car rolled to a stop in front of my building, the engine still running quietly. After a moment, the driver climbed out and raised his head toward me, casting a quick glance over the building's facade. Slightly uncomfortable on my second-floor window ledge, I looked away and began wiping distractedly, doing my best to look occupied. I wiped slowly, almost in place, my eyes downcast. "Hallo," the driver said abruptly, to attract my attention, "did you call for a taxi?" "Me?" I said, cautiously pointing at my breast with the sponge. Me? How could he accuse me? Couldn't he see I was busy washing the windows? He let it drop there. Once he'd approached the front door and pressed vainly on a number of buttons, then exchanged a few words over the hawthorn hedge with the landlord (who must still have been reading in his lawn chair, I imagine, I could only hear his voice), the driver returned to his car, again looked up at me (immediately lowering my eyes, I resumed my ostentatious wiping of the windowpane), climbed into the driver's seat and drove off. A second later, the building's front door opened below me and a young woman hurried out. She looked around her and settled in to wait, keeping a close watch on the end of the street. After a moment, as if sensing my presence behind her, she looked up and stared pensively at me from afar for a minute, her head turned in profile, gloomily biting her lower lip. I immediately looked away, wiping the windowpane with a gentle, meditative air, slow and detached, one foot raised behind me, trying to look as appealing as I could at my window (as if I really didn't care all that much about what I was doing). I don't even know if she was still looking at me. It was then, as I went on wiping my windowpane with an intelligent air, one foot raised behind me, that I heard the voice of the landlord below me, calling out to the young woman from his lawn chair. Unfortunately, I couldn't quite see his body from where I stood (except by leaning perilously out over the void, which really didn't seem worth it). He soon came into sight, however, making his way through his little garden, his book in his hand, to speak with the young woman over the hawthorn hedge, and no doubt to tell her what he knew of the taxi. I could see the two of them talking across the hedge, the landlord looking apologetic and contrite, gesturing toward the corner with one hand, and her, the young woman, listening to him in the street, her head lowered, silent, lost, very dark, very desirable (yes indeed, I said to myself, and I very gently wrung my sponge into the basin).

Now I closed the window again, and, before heading into the kitchen to stow my gear, I did a bit more tidying up in the living room, summarily dusting the couch cushions, holding them up in profile to give them a few good swats with the flat of my hand, then spraying a few bursts of cleaner in the middle of the coffee table and giving it a quick circular wipe with the sponge. Finally, just as I was about to leave the room with my spray bottle and basin under my arm, I cast a quick glance toward the television set. Noticing that it too was dusty, I gave it a carefree little shot from my bottle, and the resulting spray crashed against the top of the screen in a little wad of whitish, effervescent foam; then, feeling a slight giddiness in which the simple childish pleasure of shooting mingled with a subtler sort of delight, symbolic and intellectual, linked to the nature of my chosen target, I kept firing again and again, draining the spray bottle of almost all its detergent, firing shot after shot straight at the screen, point blank, squeezing the lever then relaxing my finger, squeezing and relaxing, faster and faster, anywhere that struck my fancy, all over the screen, until the entire surface was covered by a coating of mobile, foaming liquid, slowly slipping earthward, intermingled with grime and dust, in sluggish, oleaginous flows that seemed to ooze from the machine like the residue of programs past, melted and liquefied and rolling in waves over the glass, the livelier ones speeding down in one non-stop swoop, while others sank more slowly and ponderously to the bottom of the screen, then changed course and poured over the floor, like shit, or like blood.

Now dusk had fallen, and I sat alone in the twilight facing the dark TV set. I hadn't yet turned on the little halogen lamp beside me, and the living room was bathed in the soft, orange-hued penumbra of a summer evening. After some time, still gazing at the dark set in front of me, I noticed the part of the room I was sitting in reflected on the surface of the glass. Backward, as if seen in a convex mirror à la Van Eyck, all the room's furniture and objects seemed to converge, bulging, toward the center of the screen, with the luminous and slightly deformed lozenge of the window at the top, the dense, shadowy mass of the couch and coffee table dimly standing out from the walls, and then the finer lines, cleaner and more clearly discernible, of the halogen lamp, the radiator, and the coffee table. I recognized my own dark form in the middle of the screen, motionless on the couch. I was feeling a bit worn out, and my plan was to spend the rest of the evening at home. The best thing, in fact, and the smart thing, I told myself, would be to get into my pajamas right away and make up a TV tray (in purely theoretical terms, of course), so that I could quietly spend the rest of the evening in the living room, a blanket over my knees, preparing to take up my work again the next day.

One evening not too long ago, I attempted a curious little experiment as I was watching television. When you watch television, you're continuously made to construct your own mental picture from the three million varyingly bright points of light that the televised image puts before you, your mental activity thus constantly completing the always-in-progress configuration of the images you're being shown (which sounds like a rather complicated task, of course, but don't worry: one glance at a viewership study and you'll see it's well within anyone's grasp). That night, then, a week or two ago, I watched the evening news on German channel 2, sitting on the couch with a TV tray (happy days, now gone forever), barefoot, my hand cradling the family jewels, serenely eating a chicken leg with mayonnaise. Then, in order to see the experiment through with my character-istic rigor, I set the drumstick down on the coffee table, wiping my fingertips on a little napkin, and, never removing my eyes from the screen, my mind focused and my eye watchful, I began to count some twenty luminous points on the television screen; or rather, to put it more precisely, I located exactly zero points, but since the image of a newsreader nevertheless continued to get through to my brain, I deduced that, from the twenty-some points that I must in fact have been seeing on the screen, my mind had managed to re-constitute the entirety of the image in question, logically complet-ing it from the elements supplied, filling in the missing dots line by line to obtain a coherent, unbroken image of the bespectacled face of Jürgen Klaus, who was presenting the news on German channel 2 that evening. Then, taking a closer look at that affected, serious face made of three million points of light, still reading the evening news at fifty sweeps per second and six hundred twenty-five lines per image, I realized that the bespectacled anchorman before me wasn't Jürgen Klaus after all, but Claus Seibel. I can never quite tell one newsreader from another, in spite of the three million rainbow-hued points of light that define them.

Sometime around eight o'clock that evening, still sitting in the living room, I felt an urge to turn on the television and watch the news (but I didn't act on it, I admire that about myself). Sit-ting on the couch, legs crossed, I wondered how many of us there were who might be not watching television at this moment, and even, more broadly, how many there were of us worldwide who had given up watching television forever. Lacking any precise statistical inquiry into this question, the only more-or-less reliable criterion for membership in a category as vague and indiscernible as people who never watch television was no doubt the absence of a television in the living room. And even this wasn't an absolute criterion, since it excluded people like me, who found themselves in the paradoxical situation of owning a television and never watching it (although, for my part, I'd only given it up for good a little more than twenty-four hours before). But let's not complicate things, that changed nothing in statistical terms; besides, it's probably safe to assume that the number of people who own a television and stopped watching it less than twenty-four hours before is nothing short of infinitesimal. As for the rest, according to the few studies of this question that I'd had occasion to skim, it seems that only two to three percent of European households are not equipped with a television. Add that number to the few atypical cases like me who have a television but never watch it, and you come up with a healthy little total of three percent of the European population who are absolutely resistant to the idea of television. But then, we must note that this encouraging figure is for the most part made up of bums, street people, delinquents, prisoners, loners, and the mentally ill. For such indeed seemed the principal characteristic of the statistical category of households without televisions: to be not so much without a television as without a household.

Suddenly, rising from the couch and leaving the living room (I couldn't go on hanging around the apartment, I had to get out), I called John Dory.

I'd met John Dory a few months before, at a reading put on in a Berlin bookstore to mark the publication of a new German translation of Proust, a rather tedious affair that involved a guy sitting at a table reading Proust for almost an hour (while I sat on my plastic chair in the back of the bookstore, quiet and attentive, understanding scarcely a word of the Ostrogoth's ramblings). When the reading was over, as everyone was standing around in the bookstore, relieved, John Dory, accompanied by one of those willowy students who were his specialty (he must have met her a few hours earlier in some public place, a park or a library, and brought her to this Proust reading with as much quivering enthusiasm as if he were whisking her off to a hotel), was introduced to me by mutual friends, and we exchanged a few words as the last members of the audience slowly filed out. In the ensuing conversation, soon joined by the shop's owner, someone asked what I was doing in Berlin, and this time I wisely avoided making any explicit mention of my study of Charles V and Titien Vecellio, for fear that I might compromise its imminent inception by prematurely expounding on its themes in public. Rather, I somewhat obscurely observed how curious it was that Proust's few allusions to Titian in *Remembrance of Things*

Past refer to him sometimes as *Titien*, sometimes as *le Titien* (as if Proust himself, in other words, had remained undecided on this point right up to the end).

John Dory, whom I later met up with again once or twice, was in Berlin to work on a doctoral thesis in philosophy he'd started in Paris two years before. His subject was a hermetic, unknown American philosopher whom for my part I claimed he'd never even read, once our relationship was close enough to allow this little impertinence (but he gave me his assurances to the contrary, with a modest, persevering smile). Tessinese Swiss on his mother's side, Anglophone Canadian on his father's, John Dory had a slight, indefinable accent, more English than Italian to my Francophone ear, perhaps French to a German ear, Italian to an English ear, etc. He'd moved to Berlin a few months before, and he eked out a more-or-less decent existence by teaching English and French in various private institutions. Sometimes he gave private lessons to get through the last days of the month, or lent his assistance to a theater designer for an upcoming show. He also did some translating, literary or commercial, various little odd jobs. Thus, since the beginning of summer, John had been spending his Tuesday and Friday afternoons filling in for an analyst, Doctor Joachim von M., who'd gone away on vacation at the start of July. John once explained to me how this worked, in general very simply: he arrived at Doctor von M.'s a little before two, went upstairs to his apartment after padlocking his bicycle in the courtyard, and made coffee in the kitchen as he awaited the patients. They usually arrived at about two, and John went to show them in when they rang the bell. Most of the patients were aware of Doctor von M.'s absence and asked him no questions, entering without a word. For the very rare cases where things might go differently, Doctor von M. had advised him to answer as evasively as possible, with a simple affirmative blink or a small pensive smile signifying nothing specific, and in fact everything had always gone very smoothly so far; the patients had never given John any trouble. Hands clasped behind his back, he set off before them down the hallway and escorted them into the office. There, still asking no questions, most of the patients immediately went and stretched out on the couch while John settled into a chair, crossed his legs, and quietly waited, looking around him. The patients never need much prodding. Soon they began to speak, some haltingly, sometimes falling into long silences, others with more agitation, in painful, tortured sentences that couldn't quite come out, all this to the tick-tock of the old imitation-Biedermeier grandfather clock in one corner of Doctor von M.'s study, its long silver pendulum imperturbably keeping time. Now and then John cast a quick, furtive glance at the patient on the couch and raised his eyes to the heavens, tugging at the ends of his scarf. John didn't understand everything the patients said, of course, but that was of no particular importance, he told me; it was still good for his German, in any case, and it helped him develop his ear, as he said, to hear that unending soft murmur of grammatically irreproachable German sentences. And then of course he was under no obligation to listen to everything they said; Doctor von M. hadn't asked him for any precise account of these sessions, no transcription or list of revelations, which meant that John didn't even have to hold a notepad on his knees and take down the patients' words, which might in time have grown tiresome. At the end of the session, John stood up and saw his patients to the door, where they ritually offered him two hundred marks in cash, with the stiff, slightly shamefaced manner of those who know the symbolic meaning of money, uncomfortable at the thought of passing banknotes from hand to hand. Slipping the bills into his pocket without false modesty, John went out onto the landing with them for a moment, gave them a little good-bye wave from a distance, and, thinking "good riddance," watched them start down the stairs before he went back into Doctor von M.'s apartment and closed the door behind him. He headed into the living room, his hands in his pockets, whistling a little tune, pensively poured himself a scotch, turned on the television, and lay down on the couch to await the next neuropath. What I found most intriguing in all this was that physically John was the very image of a mental patient, with that anxious, intelligent, cunning gaze of his, sometimes aglow with a fleeting, hallucinatory fire, that ambiguous smile, that long black hair falling over his shoulders or pulled back into a ponytail, whereas the patients were for the most part such genteel sorts, mannerly and well-dressed, perhaps a little drab and dull, just as analysts themselves generally are, with Loden jackets and neatly-trimmed beards, neckties or bow-ties, and almost inevitably some extravagant little touch to personalize the ensemble, a short, over-elaborate pipe for instance, or a discreet diamond or zirconium ring on one pinky. I knew this because I'd seen several of them one day when I stood in for John at Doctor von M.'s office, one Friday afternoon when John couldn't get away and asked me to replace him at a moment's notice.

I caught John at home when I called him that evening. He wasn't doing anything in particular (he was reading, John was always reading), and I suggested we meet at around nine at the Einstein Café. Before leaving the apartment, I took a shower and washed my hair (or at least, I merrily lathered my duckling down in the shower). Then, before putting on my old pants and a fresh shirt, I treated my upper back with Biafine, a smooth, soothing cream, ideal for burns, which Delon had bequeathed to me just before she went off to Italy. I squeezed the tube to force a dab of cream onto my fingertip, oh, just a dab, and delicately smoothed it over the red, slightly ravaged skin of my shoulders, slowly rubbing in regular circles to work the cream into the epidermis before cautiously slipping on my shirt. I was really managing very well on my own; if it came to that, I might even have tried to insert a suppository by myself. But let's not get carried away, it was only a sunburn. Lost in thought, I left the apartment, checking to be sure I had my key and some money (such an anxious soul), and tranquilly started off down the stairs. I was wearing a light jacket, and that night I'd chosen to embellish my deck shoes, which are generally worn barefoot, with a pair of white socks that lent them a little touch of local color. Now I could surely pass for a real Berliner. If it weren't for my accent, of course. Still, I was under no obligation to open my mouth. A laconic Berliner, then. I boarded a double-decker bus on the Arnheimplatz, presented my monthly pass to the driver, and went up to find a seat in the front row of the upper deck. All alone in the *impériale*, my feet propped up on the window ledge, I watched the last rosy gleams of the sun fading over the city before me. The bus had just crossed the railway bridge by the Halensee S-Bahn station, and I let myself be conveyed through the streets of Berlin, thinking of my monograph, not so much concretely and methodically, reflecting on this or that precise aspect of my work, but rather in a purely beatific mode, vague and airy, blithe and aimless, as if all those marvelous unformed thoughts in my mind would one day come together in the immutable marble of an ideal, finished monograph. You can always dream.

From the outside, the Einstein Café might be mistaken for a private bourgeois house, with a gate out front and a little flight of steps leading up to the door. In the early days of the century, this was the home of a very great silent-film actress (whose name I will not speak, in homage to her art); after the war it became a popular Viennese café, with, both in its decor and in its clientele, a certain quality that might be called, if not authentically Germanic, at least vaguely Saint-Germainish. It was a pleasant and tranquil place, where I liked to have drink now and then; there were newspapers from all over the world laid out on a table by the front door, each one clasped in a long, blond-wood anti-theft rod that did indeed make them rather inconvenient to swipe. I found the place quiet when I entered that night, almost deserted, only two or three customers scattered here and there on the banquettes, reading their newspapers before a cup of coffee or a glass of wine, glancing over their half-frame glasses with a slightly cross, weary curiosity to see who it was coming in now. It was me, folks. I scanned the room in search of John; failing to find him, I strode toward the French doors, one hand in my pocket, and descended the little stairway into the garden. There I saw some fifty people dining by the light of globed candles and garden lamps, enjoying the evening's exceptional mildness. Swift and energetic, three or four waiters circulated among the tables with trays in their hands, nimbly scurrying up or down the little staircase, dressed in black vests and long white aprons that fell over their legs. Some of them met on the stairs, others stopped for a moment before a table, a large black leather wallet open in their hands to make change when a bill was being settled. I didn't spot John right away, but after a moment I saw him reading at a table a little off to one side, his head bent over his book, a faint smile of pleasure illuminating his face. He was wearing a black shirt, his hair pulled into a ponytail, which frankly I preferred when we were eating together; fully deployed, that long black mane of his underscored the restrained minimalism of my duckling down a little too emphatically for my tastes. He closed his book when he saw me approaching, and we shook hands over the table, speaking of one thing and another as I took my place across from him. I opened the menu and began to study it pensively, my legs stretched out under the table and my sock-shod feet on the gravel, in no hurry to put an end to that delicious little moment before you've chosen your dinner, a moment rather like bachelorhood, when all possibilities are still open, and none yet closed off forever. Having made my choice (a Tafelspitz, always an easy decision), I closed the menu and set it down on the table before me, then turned around for a moment to see who else was dining here tonight: a few taciturn couples, a large table of Spaniards dressed as always with the kind of refined elegance you see only in Italy anymore, a few lively snatches of their conversation audible through the din, and then, a little further on, some young men looking stylish in their hats and white jackets, sitting in a circle by the steps, already drinking their after-dinner coffee and smoking cigars, accompanied by tanned young blonde women in black strapped dresses. John picked up the bottle of Bordeaux he'd ordered while he was waiting for me and reached across to pour me a glass. "No no, no alcohol," I said, covering my glass with one hand. John looked at me, speechless, the bottle hovering over the glass, and I very matter-of-factly explained that I never drank alcohol when I was working. ("Well, for goodness' sake, you must not work much," he said.)

They brought us our Tafelspitz, thin slices of beef blanched in vegetable bouillon and accompanied by two types of sauce in two little silver cups, one a slightly sweet horseradish sauce, the other flavored with chervil, with a side of sautéed potatoes. I served myself some horseradish sauce while John took a bit of the chervil, and then we traded sauce-cups over the table. I picked up the bottle of Bordeaux and poured myself a little glass of wine (in the end, I didn't think I'd be doing any more work today). I set down the bottle and announced to John that I'd stopped watching television. John nearly spewed his first bite of Tafelspitz onto his plate, hunching over the table and shaking his fingers vigorously before his mouth, not so much out of an urgent need to respond to my revelation as because he'd burned his tongue on the sautéed potatoes. He took a piece of bread from the basket, pulled out the white center, and delicately applied it to his lips to soothe the searing pain. "How long has it been?" he finally said, touching the edge of his lips one last time with his finger, then examining its underside with distant, wary curiosity (I wonder what it was he was hoping to find). "Since yesterday," I said, "yesterday afternoon." I was curious to know what his reaction might be. Thoughtfully, without speaking a word, John picked up the bottle of wine and began to pour me some more (I insinuated a little gesture of refusal, half-hearted and vague, once my glass was full), filled his own glass as well, and put the bottle down on the table. He picked up his knife and fork and carefully cut himself another piece of Tafelspitz, dabbing it with horseradish sauce before cautiously raising it to his mouth. "Me too," he answered. "I haven't watched television for three months at least." Every time I informed someone today that I'd quit watching television, first Delon this afternoon and now John here tonight, they told me that they never watched it either. Or not much, or not anymore. In the end, nobody watched television (except me, of course).

As for John, in any case, he didn't own a television. Which didn't stop him regularly reading the TV listings in the papers, he explained over dinner; sometimes he even borrowed a set for the night when there was a show on that particularly interested him, and he'd noticed that people were always rather reluctant to lend out their television sets—their books were no problem, all you like, their records, their videocassettes, their clothes, why not, but not their televisions. Their television was sacred, and whenever he did manage to borrow one, he explained with a smile, he was always struck by the owners' distress as he prepared to go away with the set, the children almost in tears in the living room under the consoling wing of their father's arm, watching John unplug the machine and the various cords connecting it to the antenna and the VCR, then following him sadly into the hallway, heads hanging, while John, slightly slowed by the receiver dangling from his fist, stepped out onto the landing and started off down the stairs, turning around to offer his thanks and a promise to bring the set back as soon as he'd seen his show. Arriving in the building's courtyard, he put the set down on the ground for a moment to catch his breath, then returned home on foot if the friends who'd lent him the set didn't live too far away, or, if they did, carefully loaded it into a little trailer yoked to his bicycle. Thoroughly securing the set in the trailer with an elaborate network of ropes and elastic bands, he climbed onto his bicycle and pedaled serenely down the street or the bike path, the big TV set carefully braced in the trailer behind him, swaddled in old newspapers and protective rags, such that someone watching this convoy pass by down the street, someone who didn't know John, might very easily have mistaken him for a junk dealer, when in fact, taken for all in all, he was only a TV viewer.

TELEVISION

John and I were slightly drunk when we emerged from the Einstein Café. John had left me a few moments before (he climbed onto
his bicycle, and I watched him pedal off into the night), and now
I was waiting all alone for a taxi on the Kurfürstenstrasse. Across
the street, a bustier-clad amazon stood in the glow of a streetlight,
her hips and thighs bare under the fine silk of her stockings, and I
tried to adopt a studious air as I stood facing her from my sidewalk.
From time to time, still watching for a hypothetical taxi at the end
of the street, I couldn't help casting a furtive glance at that half-
naked girl across the way in the dark, but, despite the very slight
drunkenness blanketing my temples, I felt no particular physical
attraction to her, not that she was ugly or not ugly, that wasn't the
question; at this distance she was non-existent, faceless and without identity, entirely encased in the most stereotypical image of
her function, only a body, svelte, blonde, and athletic, wrapped in
a wealth of erotic ornaments as apparently arousing as they were
sadly conventional, a tight-fitting bustier, a cheap little red leather
jacket, discouragingly cold and clinical. Maybe if she were a little plumper, I said to myself, and dressed in a simple translucent
nightgown, there on the sidewalk across from me, I wouldn't rule
out the possibility that I might want to cross the street, my libido
sharpened by drink, and offer her some money to let me rub against
her, fondling her breasts and caressing her hips and pussy, raising
the hem of her nightgown. For now, though, I stayed where I was,
meekly awaiting my taxi. What a contrast, sometimes, between
the ordinary taxi you're waiting for and the funny little sexual fan-

tasies that come into your mind. Her hips and her pussy, for goodness' sake! Why her hips, anyway? I wondered (as for her pussy, that made more sense to me).

The girl was still coming and going on the curb before me, now and then making an about-face, chewing her gum and swinging her little purse, spinning it nonchalantly at the end of its long gilded chain, a tiny *baise-en-ville* that in all likelihood held nothing more than a compact and a jumbled assortment of condoms and chewing gum. Eventually, since after all I'd been standing in her field of vision for some time now, with my choirboy air and my fascist socks in my deck shoes, she bent her head to one side and sent a coaxing little smile my way, just to see. Receiving no response (in any case, I didn't have a car, I wasn't trying to be difficult), she shrugged, turned around, and walked off down the sidewalk, punctiliously wiggling her little epicentral ass in my direction so that I could see in action just what I was letting slip through my fingers. But a moment later she had to interrupt this little parade, for now a car had pulled to a stop beside her in the street. Slowly retracing her steps with a disdainful sway in her hips, she approached the passenger side, still chewing her gum, bent down to lower her head into the window from atop her endless silk-encased legs, and began to chat, leaning on the door, the upper half of her body almost completely disappearing into the car as she conversed with the driver. I watched discreetly from a distance, still waiting for my taxi, wondering what on earth those two lovebirds could be talking about at such length (but no doubt I'd be disappointed if I found out, I told myself, better to go on tranquilly imagining the most debauched indecencies than be disillusioned by the undoubtedly sordid reality). Then, still pursuing the negotiations, she finally opened the door and climbed into the car, decisively slamming the door behind her. Slowly the car started off again, and for a moment I kept my eyes on its glowing red taillights as they disappeared into the night. I was still vainly awaiting my taxi on the Kurfürstenstrasse, and now I mused a little sadly on the girl who'd just gone away, on what she was going to do tonight and what she'd done today. Because what do whores do between tricks, if not watch television?

It must have been almost two o'clock in the morning when the taxi dropped me off in front of my building. There were no lights shining in the windows, only a few patches of moonlight glowing here and there, glinting off the windowpanes. On the second floor, behind the dark stone projection of the balcony, I realized the French door in my study was open. The slightly grainy facade around it looked gray in the darkness, patchily illuminated by the streetlights. On the third floor, just above my balcony, the broad double-glazed windows of the Dreschers' apartment lay in a row, and, standing there on the sidewalk, my head raised to look at the building, my eye fell on their bedroom window (my God, the fern, I suddenly said to myself). There wasn't a sound to be heard in the Dreschers' apartment when I went in that night to check on the fern's condition, and there was a certain stuffiness to the air in the entryway. The sun must have shone on the windows all day, and a heavy, stifling heat had built up in the apartment. Even the

Dreschers' odor, usually rather discreet, scarcely perceptible in my previous visits, seemed to have spread freely through the rooms in the course of the afternoon, as if, in the heat, it had finally come unstuck from the walls and curtains, the slightly grimy upholstery of the armchairs, and the wool of the carpet, where it must have been idly macerating for years, happily mingling its pungency with the molding plaster and the eroding wallpaper. Heady and fascinating, dangerous in the way that the odor of tulle can be when you surreptitiously press it to your nostrils and inhale its perfume with mingled terror and delight, the Dreschers' odor now stank freely in every room of the apartment, merry and unhindered (as if the Dreschers had come back from their vacation tonight in my absence). Slightly disturbed by this thought in spite of myself, I hastily filled my watering can from the kitchen faucet and hurried back down the hallway to make sure I was alone in the apartment. I paused for a moment outside their bedroom door, straining to hear any squeaks that might be coming from the bedsprings (a fine sight I would have made there, hovering outside the door with my watering can), and very gently opened the door, fearing in spite of everything that I might find the Dreschers naked in a tangle of sheets on their bed, like something out of a painting by Fragonard (or rather, let's be realistic, like Edward Kienholz's *While Visions of Sugarplums Danced in Their Heads*). Happily, I found no one there, and I stepped gingerly into the darkness toward the fern (well, now, let's just see if the soil has rehydrated, I said to myself as I crouched down by the basin).

Carefully, with great delicacy, I inserted one finger into the mound of dirt and began to feel around as the fancy struck me, lifting up here, pushing in there. It wasn't dry dry dry, no; let's just say that I'd known more encouraging mounds (don't worry, I'm not going to name names). I'll be frank, I was a touch disappointed: there was a certain lack of viscosity, that's what it was, an absence of slickness and cohesion, of musk and civet. And then there were the fronds, disturbingly pale, sadly limp and listless compared to the lusty, vivacious vision Inge had revealed to me the day she showed me the sights. I gave the poor thing a sad little caress, brushing the back of my hand along the fronds cascading over the edge of the pot, and, taking it out of its basin, I set it down before me on the carpet. Kneeling on the floor, my watering-can beside me, I looked at the wretched plant in the dim light and wondered if, rather than proceed directly to a massive watering and run the risk of inflicting a final chill that might prove fatal to its faded charms, it might not be better to try repotting it outright, which is to say, taking great care not to damage the dense network of rootlets that clung to the side of the pot, fragile as venules, to try gently separating the main root mass into two or three smaller and more manageable ones, which I could then put into several smaller pots to rehydrate, or glasses, I don't know (such a complicated business), whatever I could find in the Dreschers' kitchen, even fancy porcelain teacups, like cuttings, if you like, but bigger than cuttings, multiplying the root systems in a sense, and dividing the stems.

I went off to water the other plants in the Dreschers' apartment, lingering for a moment in Uwe's study, my watering can in my hand. I trailed a finger over the computer, I picked up a few letters from Uwe's desk. His mail was copious, carefully sorted and classified in a folder. I examined the books and journals lying on the table, most of them dealing with administrative law in English and German, financial journals, reports, audits. Uwe was a business attorney and a politician (Uwe Drescher—maybe you've heard of him? He was a rising star in the small, sinking liberal party). All alone in the study, I slowly approached the balcony door and absently looked out the window for a moment. The moon shone over the rooftops, and here and there I could still see a distant lamp glowing in the darkness. On the balcony, bathed in the gentle light of the moon, the shadow of a folding chair rested against the wall, with a little spade and a rake leaning against it, and two or three sacks of peat lined up along the side. A planter ran the length of the railing, and, looking at that planter facing me there in the night, I reflected, despondency slowly settling over me, that I hadn't watered the daisy seedlings even once since the beginning of summer. I opened the door and went out onto the balcony to have a look at the seedlings: from one end of the planter to the other, the soil had become a cracked and arid crust, lunar or desert-like, with what must once have been a promising generation of young daisies now reduced to withered vegetal remains, blasted by the sun, what was left of their stalks drooping and limp, collapsed, as if irradiated where they stood in the scorched earth. I raised my watering can to give them a drink all the same, but I stopped myself a half-moment later (I had to throw up my hands); there was nothing more to be done, and I had no more strength to give. A dark day for the botanical world.

I rested my elbows on the railing, my watering can at my feet, and stood quietly looking at the dark summer sky. A handful of scattered stars shone tremblingly on the horizon, and I felt a closeness to those distant glimmers, those fragile, indecisive little points flickering out and coming back to life in the sky. Alone in the Berlin night, leaning on the railing of the Dreschers' balcony, I reflected on the workday now drawing to a close, and I wondered what, in the end, was the definition of a successful day's labor. Such success, if indeed it can be measured, certainly couldn't be judged quantitatively by the number of pages one might have written, nor, it seemed to me, by the quality and scope of the more basic groundwork one might have laid. No, the best criterion for evaluating the success of a day's work, it seemed to me, was surely the way we have seen the time pass as we worked, the singular capacity the hours have demonstrated to take on the weight of our work, associated with the apparently contradictory impression that the time has flown by at great speed, heavy with the work we've accomplished, laden with that work's meaning, charged with all the experiences we've gone through, and yet so incomparably light that we never so much as noticed it passing. That's what grace is, it seemed to me, that mix of fullness and lightness, which you can only experience in certain privileged moments of your existence, moments of writing or love.

I'd headed back into the Dreschers' apartment, and now I was distractedly looking at the books on the shelves in their bedroom. I'd lit one little lamp on a bedside table, and I stood silently turning the pages of a book I'd taken down from a shelf. When I was done, I put it back in its place and went to sit on the Dreschers' bed. The television stood silent before me on a little black stand holding several stacks of videocassettes, some in black plastic cases, others bare, with a simple homemade label stuck to the side to announce the title of the film or program it contained. I stood up for a look out the bedroom window. The street below lay deserted under the streetlights, and I stood motionless by the window, my hands in my pockets, staring at the building across the way, where all the lights were now off. Everyone in Berlin was sleeping. Somewhat hesitantly, slowly retracing my steps, I picked up the remote control from the top of the television and turned on the set.

In my own mind, of course, it went without saying that the decision to stop watching television in no way applied outside my own home.

Because surely the fact that I'd decided to stop watching television should not be construed to mean that I must now cut myself off from the world around me, and that, should I for instance find myself one evening in the home of some friends and spy a television set turned on in the living room, I would be obligated to cover my eyes in my armchair so as not to break my word, or that, should I

be walking down the street one day and pass by a shop with television sets turned on in the window, I would immediately have to
cross the street to avoid violating my oath. No. No such tartuffer-
ies for me. There was no intellectual inflexibility in my attitude,
scarcely a trace of ostentation in my method. I'd stopped watching
television, granted, but this in no way implied that I would now
have to force myself into all sorts of ridiculous contortions in my
day-to-day life. I would even say, without attempting to draw up a
complete list of all the little exceptions that I thought I could permit myself without in any way transgressing my rule (this being
my own little way of tempering the Jansenism of my self-imposed
laws, allowing a certain pliability in their application), that if some
great sporting event might be scheduled in the months or years to
come, something rare and exceptional in nature, I'm thinking of
the Olympic Games for instance, the finals of the 100-meter race
in the Olympic Games, I couldn't quite see why, in the name of
what narrow-minded purism, intransigent and abstract, I would
have to deprive myself of those ten little seconds of air time (ten
seconds! not even that!).

And so I lay distractedly watching television on the Dreschers'
bed. It was a bit dark in the bedroom, and the oblique cone of light
emanating from the screen mingled in the dimness with the filtered glow of the little bedside lamp I'd turned on. I stuffed a pillow behind my back and, my legs crossed on the blanket, I slowly
changed channels, one to the next, tapping on the remote control.
I'd turned down the volume to avoid disturbing the neighbors (I

put myself in my place, suppose I'd been trying to sleep one floor below), which meant that I could now hear virtually nothing (and I couldn't understand much of the German before, anyway). I looked at all those men and women absorbed in their midnight discussions in their various studios as if it were the most natural thing in the world, smiling, their legs crossed, and from time to time I cut off their prattle with a simple push of one finger on the remote control, moving on to other silent debaters explaining who knows what, their fingers trembling with nerves. I thus flitted from one nocturnal roundtable to another, from series to movie clip, changing channels with no particular motive, almost mechanically, for no reason, the way you scratch your back in the summertime, or the back of your thigh, from German channels to Turkish channels, national channels to local channels, government-subsidized channels to commercial channels, some of them devoted to a specific theme, others requiring payment, coded, encrypted (or, to blur the movies, quivering black and white horizontal lines accompanied by a metallic insect scritching). Reaching the end of the numbered channels, in those abyssal, mysterious nether reaches of the Hertzian network, where enigmatic snow-filled screens lay abandoned in the night, I sometimes even landed on a test-pattern, one of those test-patterns whose primary vocation was in theory to announce the end of the day's broadcast, which should at long last have offered some respite from this endless procession of channels and shows, a pause, some time to breathe before the programs started up again the next day; but these very test-patterns themselves had been endowed with life and movement so as to transmit still more images, still more sounds (in contrast to the poignant, fixed image of the anticipatory test-patterns of yesteryear, which to my wondering childlike eyes announced the imminent start of the delayed broadcast of that day's stage of the Tour de France), still more motion, hurried and frantic, breathlessly and unstoppably accelerating like that haunting subjective shot filmed from an S-Bahn locomotive racing over the tracks in the suburbs of Berlin.

Television is formal beyond all reason, I now told myself as I lay on the Dreschers' bed; twenty-four hours a day, it seems to flow along hand in hand with time itself, aping its passage in a crude parody where no moment lasts and everything soon disappears, to the point where you might sometimes wonder where all those images go once they've been broadcast, with no one watching them or remembering them or retaining them, scarcely seen at all, only momentarily skimmed by the viewer's gaze. For where books, for instance, always offer a thousand times more than they are, television offers exactly what it is, its essential immediacy, its ever-evolving, always-in-progress superficiality.

Before leaving the Dreschers' apartment, I entered the kitchen to set the fern pot to soak in the sink for the rest of the night. Then, still standing there indecisively, a bit unsure of my next move, I opened the refrigerator to see what I might find inside (a little bottle of beer would have been nice). Crouching down before the appliance, my fist clutching the door handle, I examined the brightly-lit interior, contrasting somewhat with the gentle dimness blanketing the kitchen. There was nothing much of note in the refrigerator apart from a half-eaten, dried-out jar of mustard on the shelf in the door. Other than that the racks were bare, except for a bottle of Sekt wrapped in tissue paper, lying horizontally on one of the grillwork shelves. I took out the bottle, examined it for a moment in my hands, and, taking care not to tear it, lifted the tissue paper for a look at the label. I put the bottle back. A delicious coolness poured from the refrigerator, almost palpable, like hesitant, visible billows of iced condensation bathing my face in that pool of light. I rose to my full height again, turned around to look at the fern in the sink, thought for a moment. To tell the truth, I was a little worried about the Dreschers. My fear was that they might find my attitude rather cavalier, returning home from vacation to find their fern in this state after entrusting it to me for the summer. I gave one of the fronds a sad, half-hearted caress with one finger, lifting a leaf and letting it fall again. Seeing the plant so weak, so limp, so resigned, I then conceived the idea of subjecting it to a kind of shock therapy. I picked up the pot and put it in the refrigerator, just over the vegetable drawer. I closed the door and listened for a moment. No reaction, nothing, just the refrigerator's simple, unbroken hum resonating in the kitchen.

Now I was back in the Dreschers' room, watching television. I'd stopped flipping through the channels for a moment, lingering lazily on a women's team-handball game, no doubt a delayed broadcast (I didn't think it very likely that these young women were actually playing handball at this hour). In any case, delayed or not, a goal had just been scored, and the players were all running back to their side, resuming their positions on the field, giving each other encouraging little pats on the shoulder, calling out plays to each other (Bayer Leverkusen was up seventeen to fourteen). Thoughtful, my legs crossed on the bed, I watched all this absentmindedly, vaguely imagining one of the players naked beneath her strapped suit, more or less passively, with no real investigatory effort, not trying to determine, for instance, on the basis of the few concrete elements of her anatomy distinguishable on the screen—her complexion, the very faint downy shadow on her upper lip or the fine hairs on her forearms—just what the actual nudity of this young woman might look like, nor making the truly minimal effort of closing my eyes for a moment and taking the trouble, if it wasn't asking too much, to imagine her naked and sweating on the field. And yet that's the best way to watch television actively: with your eyes closed.

Then I began to wonder why exactly I'd stopped watching television. Still sitting there facing the screen (eighteen to fourteen now, a fine goal by the Bayer Leverkusen replaying in slow motion), I mused that, if Delon had put that question to me this afternoon, or John this evening at the restaurant, I probably couldn't have come up with an answer. No doubt my decision to stop watching television had its roots in a whole complex of reasons, all of them necessary, none sufficient, and it would be pointless, I think, to seek one single motivation for the step I'd taken. Someone once told me of a reporter for an American network who'd managed to interview some desperate soul moments after he'd shot himself in the head; the reporter inquired into the reasons behind this gesture (the tape was very crudely shot, a bit dim, a bit blurry, in high documentary style, the cameraman had knelt down on the ground, his camera on his shoulder, and the reporter had simply brought his microphone to the poor fellow's mouth and carefully slipped his hand behind his nape to raise his head, so that, if he wanted to speak, he could speak into the microphone), and apparently the wretch, lying on the sidewalk in a pool of blood, feebly raising his hand heavenward in the manner of both Plato's August pose in *The School of Athens* and the more enigmatic gesture of Leonardo da Vinci's *Saint John the Baptist*, painfully extended the middle finger of his right hand toward the camera and murmured, "Fuck you."

For the moment, I decided I might stick to that same explanation, and I turned off the television.

For the next few days, I no longer tried to work quite so systematically on my monograph, preferring to adopt a more subterranean mode of attack, less overt, more diffuse. I rose in the morning at about nine o'clock, maybe nine-thirty, then took the bus to Grunewald forest for a long walk. Little by little, I'd even started going to the pool again. I'd bought some little blue rubber swimming goggles, light and streamlined, with two separate portholes of transparent plastic, like bifocal lenses, which left me with a pair of huge, staring eyes when I pulled them down onto my nose to swim and gave me a romantic motorcyclist look when I pushed them up onto my forehead as I climbed out of the water. Walking along the edge of the pool, my arms hanging limp, a towel over my shoulder, I returned to the dressing room in my swimsuit, my goggles on my forehead, now and then passing a lifeguard who sat on a stool idly staring at his feet or at some very young girl cautiously trotting along to join her friends in the din of the pool. It was difficult to say how many hundredths of a second I might have shaved off my lap time with these professional goggles enhancing my naturally aquadynamic hairstyle (a very close and downy crop), because I'd discovered that I really wasn't very good at swimming underwater. The water always ended up finding its way into my nose, if not my mouth, when I frantically raised my head, low on oxygen and perilously close to suffocating, for a desperate mouthful of air that almost inevitably went down the wrong way and left me gasping and coughing in the middle of the pool. Thus, for the most part I simply went on swimming in my usual tranquil manner, my head bobbing over the surface, my glasses pushed up onto my forehead (the classic professor in a library, in short).

I was one of a little group of regulars at the pool, who, while never going so far as to greet each other, much less fall into conversation, came for a dip at about the same hour each morning, and found in the regularity of these meetings the rather pathetic source of a small satisfaction, judging at least by my own feelings (but then I'm a bit sentimental). Slowly I extended my arms in the clear water, surrounded by familiar faces, one a gentleman I'd seen the day before, another an old woman whose flowered bonnet I recognized with a little surge of heartwarmed gratitude, a little islet of stability, unchanging and reassuring, deep in the heart of a city that has known such turmoil over, say, the last eighty years. Concentrating on the simple natural sequence of my movements, I swam peacefully in the blue-tinged water, reflecting on the evolution of my work, swimming never having seemed to me incompatible with scholarship, quite the reverse. Reflected glints of sunlight skipped amiably along beside me, multiple, rainbow-hued, refracted, shimmering along my arms with every stroke, and so, pursuing my pool-lengths, I continued to work peacefully on my monograph. There are always two distinct processes in any literary endeavor, it seems to me, two separate poles, complementary in a way, but requiring two diametrically opposed qualities. The first, subterranean, is a gestational process, demanding looseness and flexibility, a game and open mind, in order to fuel the handling of new ideas and new materials, while the second is soberer, more orderly, requiring method and discipline, austerity and rigor; this is the process that takes over when it comes time to put the text into its definitive form. Let's say that since the beginning of the summer, of those two poles, one Jansenist, the other free-flowing, I'd been favoring the more free-flowing one.

A few multicolored bath towels lay drying in the sun by the picture window. Opened wide in the summertime, the pool's big window offered a view of an abandoned soccer field in the distance, an expanse of mostly bare soil, rutted and stony, sometimes completely snow-covered in wintertime. I'd even watched a night game there one evening last winter. I'd gone to the pool a little later than usual, and I found myself almost alone in the water, tranquilly doing my lengths, now and then casting a glance through the glass into the darkness, where, in a thick layer of fog now and then whipped by sudden gusts of whirling snow, I could make out some twenty distant and indistinct forms running through the night, some of them in gloves and caps, some in black or yellow jerseys, or sometimes red, emerging from the fog, scrambling this way and that in the murky glow of the floodlights, racing over the snowy ground, slipping and sliding in pursuit of the ball, struggling to dislodge it from the mud puddles where it lay becalmed, slowed and weighed down by the mud and melted snow soaking into the leather. I swam all alone in the misty warmth of that deserted swimming pool, lit from the ceiling by two rows of fluorescent lights, while, on the other side of the glass, in the dark, glacial winter night, I could see snowflakes being swept along in slow motion by the wind, silently lighting on the windowpanes, melting on contact. In shorts and a white shirt, a thin, slouching lifeguard was putting away a few last life-rings by the water's edge, a long pole in his hand, and warning me that the pool would soon be closing.

The pool was always quiet in the summertime, never more than ten of us in the water at a time, and there was no need to look out for the other bathers as I swam; everyone in that little band of regulars was as careful to keep away from the others as they were not to make waves in the water. Sometimes, as I was swimming this way, my goggles on my forehead, thinking of my monograph, I would hear the locker-room door swing open beside me, and, automatically raising my eyes for a glimpse of the newcomer, just as you glance up from your book in the library to look at the young woman who's just walked in, following her with a dreamy gaze for a moment, briefly falling in love with her (then going back to your book with a sigh), I spotted with a twinge of displeasure what we have no choice but to call a crawler. I kept my eyes on that gentle, apparently inoffensive young man (shoulders like a clothes hanger, tiny black bathing suit) as he slowly walked the length of the pool to take his place on the starting block of his chosen lane, carefully adjusted his goggles (calmly and deliberately raising both hands to pull them down over his eyes) and suddenly cast off in an impeccable dive, followed by a silent, torpedo-like underwater advance, very disturbing in itself, but which then inevitably gave way to an explosion of perfectly synchronized activity from this weirdo's four limbs, brutal, regular, and cyclonic, and so he skimmed past me, Scud-like, leaving a churning, foamy wake that ruined my concentration for good and upset the very water itself.

After the pool I went to buy a newspaper, and often I found myself having breakfast in a nearby café. Even though it was sometimes past noon, I usually ordered one of those copious breakfasts you find in Berlin, with cold cuts and cheeses, a soft-boiled egg, orange juice, croissants, and a wicker basket holding an array of delicious, crunchy rolls, rye or wheat or bran or raisin, some of them round and split down the middle like a real French *pistolet*, others small, bulging, oblong, as if for a sandwich, tender and white inside, with a wonderful golden crust. I ate breakfast at more or less any time of the day or night in Berlin, at dawn if I hadn't gone to bed the night before, or very early in the morning, or late in the morning, or at the cocktail hour (often I lunched on breakfast). One rainy day, my favorite café was particularly packed, and more people were coming in all the time to get out of the downpour, closing and shaking their umbrellas behind them on the threshold before stepping inside. A young woman appeared at the door and cast a quick circular glance around the room; after a moment she rather tentatively approached my table, pointing with great circumspection at the two seats beside me, on one of which my backpack sat stuffed with damp swimming things, my swimsuit and towel. She quickly reeled off a long interrogative sentence in German to ask if she might sit down here. Somewhat flustered, I said yes, no, go ahead, don't hesitate, my head and my hands working together, like one of those Buddhas with a thousand eyes and a thousand arms, all of them moving at once to invite her to sit down, cordially, briskly clearing away my backpack and shifting my newspapers, briefly smoothing my hair, and she sat down at my table. I smiled at her, surprised, flattered, befuddled, slid my cup and my little coffee pot toward my end of the table, pulled my plate of cheese and meats toward me to give her more room. I was just about to attack my soft-boiled egg, but there was no hurry, no hurry. Eating a soft-boiled egg never shows you to your best advantage. So experienced with women. So savvy. I waited, my little spoon in my hand. I had time, I could wait. She pulled off her scarf, shaking her hair to let it fall over her shoulders, then stood up to doff her sodden trench coat, which she went and hung up on a coat rack some distance away. I looked on, pensively admiring her elegant, high-cut Dacron trousers, the waistband delicately encircling her waist. We weren't allowed to pursue this little adventure much further, though, for already a man was entering the café, tall, elegant, and well-built, in a black polo shirt and a gray jacket, his air decisive, his hair wavy. With a quick flutter of her hand she caught his eye and beckoned him to my table, where she'd found two places free. Wordlessly approaching, he sat down beside me, tugging at the crease of his trousers, blinked a quick greeting, picked up the menu, opened it, and began to read it attentively. Moving a little to one side, I gave him a discreet glance (and, what can you do, I launched into my soft-boiled egg).

One day as I was leaving the pool in the late morning, my backpack agape as I stowed my towel and goggles, I decided to go home on foot and take advantage of the fine sunny weather. Somehow, in these last few days of July, Berlin made me think of Paris in August. Here and there, at the four corners of vast, gray, deserted intersections, the stoplights went from green to red meaning nothing to anyone, occasionally immobilizing some lone pedestrian, patient and obedient, who, with that exemplary Northern civility, waited for the light to turn green before setting out alone into the roadway. Sometimes, more out of distraction than mischievous-

ness, lost in the play of the complex and delectable little reflections
I spun out as I walked (I could work on my monograph almost as
well walking as swimming), I involuntarily led some old woman
into error, stopping for a moment at the red light across from her,
less out of respect for the rather prissy and puerile convention of
the color of the lights than as a way of punctuating my thought,
a chance to give it an abrupt, fleeting change of direction before
I resolutely set off again, regally indifferent to the color of the
light, of course, but for that very reason leading the old woman
into error, for she would then step into the street along with me,
imitatively as it were, caught up in my own momentum, my own
propulsion, wrongly interpreting my step forward as a clear sign
that the light had turned green. I thus crossed intersections at the
risk of old women's lives (sometimes, rarely, a sudden, strident
squeal of brakes erupted behind me). Back at home, in the cool,
shady vestibule of my building, the heavy cast-iron door propped
open with a little wooden wedge, a smell of soap and wet stone
in the air, I found I had mail: two letters and a large padded envelope that wouldn't fit into the mailbox, left by the mailman in a
conspicuous spot. I quickly glanced at the two letters, green en-
velopes of no interest marked with the logo of my bank; I looked
more closely at the large padded envelope, sent from Italy, having immediately recognized Delon's handwriting. Clutching my
backpack between my knees, I opened it on the spot and pulled out
several dozen papers of various sizes, a complete collection of my
son's latest drawings. After reading Delon's note in the lobby with
a tender smile, I examined my son's drawings one after another.

They were magnificent (and I'm not just saying that because he's my son). The majority were executed in colored felt-tip, except one more complicated drawing that incorporated a number of substances I couldn't quite define, jam maybe, or veal liver, and a little piece of crushed corn-flake still stuck to the bottom. My favorite drawing was called *This Is Batman Resting*, which I assumed to be an allegorical representation of his father. I was holding it before me at arm's length to admire it when a car pulled up and quietly parked in the street outside. I turned my head, *Batman Resting* in my hand, and spotted the Dreschers, home from vacation.

Inge (I was still standing motionless in the entryway, observing the car from a distance) had a deep tan, and I watched her open the door and get out of the car. Equally tanned, Uwe was wearing a summery short-sleeved polo shirt, as well as his scholarly little round tortoise-shell glasses. He still had his car keys in his hand, and, standing on the sidewalk, his trousers rumpled from the journey, he was gazing at his car with a weary look, wondering how to go about unloading it. Still observing them from a distance out of the corner of my eye (I'd stepped back by the mailboxes to take refuge in the shadows), I considered my wisest course of action, whether to disappear into my apartment as quickly as I could or, on the contrary, to go meet them at once and surprise them with a friendly welcome at the very moment of their return. I opted for the latter solution, and, emerging from the shadows, I advanced toward the street, slipping my son's drawings back into the padded envelope. Inge spotted me first. She hurried trippingly to meet me, lay a hand on my shoulder, and gave me a rather clumsy air-kiss that let our lips graze for an instant. Uwe, on her heels, seemed briefly tempted to imitate her, in celebration of our reunion; but he stiffened as I approached, awkwardly breaking his momentum, aborting his forward propulsion at the moment of its launch, and this, coupled with my own hesitation as he came forward to meet me, culminated in an awkwardly choreographed formal embrace, as ungainly as it was neighborly.

Still clutching my big padded envelope, I offered to help the Dreschers unload their car, and the three of us peered into the open trunk with some skepticism. In the interstices of a precise arrangement of bags and suitcases, a few smaller objects, diverse and heterogeneous, had found their niche: two tennis rackets in their old-fashioned plaid sheaths, a carrying-case for a video camera, a Jokari set. Standing back a little from the other two, I sought out some not-too-heavy item that I could carry to my own advantage, preferably something voluminous and light, an eiderdown in its wrapper for instance, and, carefully moving aside a heavy suitcase, I leaned forward to extract an old blue leather golf bag with an assortment of old, mismatched clubs. I hoisted it out, slung it over my shoulder, and set off, the golf bag strapped over my chest. Uwe preceded me down the hawthorn-lined walkway with two enormous, absurdly heavy suitcases that he seemed to have great difficulty carrying, no doubt full of books (he must have spent the summer rereading *The Thibaults*), while Inge walked beside me, a large canvas bag and a few magazines in her hand, her eyes raised toward the building's sun-splashed facade. "What beautiful weather you're having here," she said. "We weren't so lucky." "Where were you?" I asked, and I slowed down to let her go through the doorway ahead of me. "At Le Zoute," she said. "Le Zoute?" I said. "Le Zoute," she said, "do you know it?" "You were at Knokke-le-Zoute?" I said. I couldn't believe it. The Dreschers had spent their vacation at Knokke-le-Zoute (they'd just come back from that very spot). They'd rented a large house with a swimming pool in the residential neighborhood behind the sea wall. It was one of their friends, a Flemish politician, who'd introduced them to the Belgian coastline, Uwe explained; he'd invited them to his villa a few years before, and since then they've gone every summer, having taken a liking to the resort's charms, the thalassotherapy at La Réserve, the promenades, the tennis, the golf. This year, when unfortunately it never stopped raining, explained Uwe, a little out of breath, stopping in the lobby to open his mailbox and take out his mail, they'd brought thick sweaters and windbreakers and had gone for long mountain-bike rides in the Flemish countryside, all the way to Bruges, even, by little district roads, along the canals and the towpaths, a wonderful little outing, he told me, and he set off again, starting up the stairs before me, they weren't sorry they went, they did it together, along with a Portuguese delegate to the European Parliament and his wife ("Oh, yes, that must have been great," I said). Once inside his apartment, Uwe dropped the two huge suitcases on the carpet, exaggerating his gesture rather than trying to minimize it, and, hurrying out again right away, went down to fetch the last suitcases from the car while Inge came in and put down her bag in the entryway. She opened the door to Uwe's study, and I followed her in. We pensively looked around the study together, saying nothing. Then, as she was about to open the door onto the balcony, I resolved to take the bull by the horns and announced in low tones that the daisy seedlings had suffered a small heatstroke and unfortunately hadn't pulled through, that they were in fact dead. She didn't seem overly affected by this sad news; she only nodded in compassionate memory of the poor seedlings, trailing a pensive finger over the dried earth in the planter. I stood motionless at her side on the balcony and glanced toward her, slightly uncomfortable (she looked at me too, furtively). I'd rested my elbows on the railing beside her, the golf bag slung over my shoulder, and we stood side by side, her hair fluttering in the breeze, softly brushing my face.

Unloading the car below us as we looked on, Uwe pulled out the last two suitcases, locked the trunk, and started off down the hawthorn-lined walk toward the building. Apparently sensing that he was being watched, he raised his eyes, his two hands busy with the suitcases, and, seeing us side by side on the third floor, he gave us a clenched little hello with his chin. I immediately returned his greeting, scarcely moving my hand, as one does from a balcony in response to a crowd's acclamations. After a moment, far briefer than I would have thought (I would never have imagined he could climb two flights of stairs so quickly with two suitcases of such weight), he appeared on the balcony to join us, quite breathless, very calm, his gaze somber and steady, one hand in his pocket, and he went and stood beside Inge, discreetly putting an arm around her waist. Then, as we made our way into the living room, Uwe walking down the hallway ahead of us among the many green plants they'd left in my care, I noted with pleasure what a wonderful summer the yucca had had, and Inge apparently noticed it too, discreetly caressing its spike as she passed by, whispering some ribald little pleasantry to it in German. We settled into the living room (I rid myself of the golf bag, cautiously leaning it against the wall with both hands, there we go, to be sure it wouldn't slip and fall to the ground). Inge sat down on the couch beside me, tugging at the hem of her skirt and smiling at me. She seemed delighted to be back home with her plants, and, looking around her, very much the lady of the house, she said with a smile that she was sorry she couldn't offer us all anything to drink, since they'd only got home a moment before; but then, thinking, placing a finger against her temple, she remembered that there must still be a bottle of Sekt in the refrigerator. "I'll go and get it," she said, rising joyously from the couch. "No! No," I cried, and I clutched at her arm to prevent her from taking another step. Immediately releasing her arm and getting hold of myself, I told her it wasn't worth opening a bottle of Sekt, I really wasn't thirsty (it had just flashed through my mind that the fern pot was still in the refrigerator).

For a moment the Dreschers looked at me in bewilderment. My shout had clearly cast a pall. Inge slowly sat down again on the edge of the couch, her movements almost visibly broken down into discrete sequences. After a long and painfully thoughtful silence, Uwe raised his eyes and looked at me with a blend of close attention

and concerned curiosity. "You're not thirsty?" he said. "No, no, really, you're very kind, but," I answered, vigorously waving my hand
before me in a gesture of refusal (what must I have been like when I
was thirsty?). Eventually Uwe stood up, still preoccupied, and took a
few steps across the room, stopping at the golf bag and touching the
clubs, very slowly rotating the heads. He turned around and gave me
another pensive look. I sensed that my explanation had only half con-
vinced him. No, he must have suspected there was something more
to all this, some hidden wound no doubt, some secret grief, perhaps
linked to alcohol, since it was the offer of a drink that had provoked
my outburst. Maybe he was imagining I'd had a little problem with
alcohol in the past, and that now, having stopped drinking, I sensed
danger when the possibility of opening a bottle of Sekt was raised,
which would explain the clumsy violence of my refusal. Well, who
knows, you never can tell with people (once again, the reality of the
situation was much simpler than that: it's just that I'd left a fern in
my upstairs neighbors' refrigerator).

And, still sitting on the Dreschers' couch, silent and pensive,
I tried to come up with some simple and discreet way of entering
the kitchen to take the fern from the refrigerator without attracting
their notice. Finally I stood up, put my right hand into my trouser
pocket (they must have thought I was about to leave), and asked if I
could use their bathroom. Hoping to minimize any outlandishness
they might find in my request, I casually added that I was only going
to pee, nothing more, obviously. The Dreschers watched me stride
away, dumbfounded, making no response, and slowly I headed off

toward the bathroom, my hand slightly clenched in my pocket, next to my thigh (I had a sense that I was sinking ever further in). Once in the bathroom, I hastily closed the door and stood listening behind it, my ear straining to catch any sound from outside, no matter how faint. I heard the Dreschers speaking quietly in the living room, probably about me (I imagined myself in their place). Then, hearing nothing more but a few distant noises, suitcases being emptied perhaps, or armoires being opened and closed, I decided to very quietly open the door and discreetly make my way into the kitchen; but no sooner had I opened it a crack than I closed it again at once, for I'd spotted Uwe's silhouette in the hallway, advancing in my direction with a suitcase to be put away in the closet next to the laundry room. I don't know if he'd spotted my little maneuver, my sudden, inept opening and closing of the door, one-two, like the fleeting beat of a butterfly's wing, but I realized that I was now completely surrounded, with Inge on one side in the living room and Uwe on the other in the laundry room. I locked the door, turning the key twice (just to be sure). I headed toward the toilet and opened the little dormer window that gave onto the building's interior courtyard. I pushed it open a crack, just enough to glimpse Uwe's shadow moving within the frame of the laundry room window. The shadow then disappeared, and, simultaneously, I heard Uwe's footsteps again in the hall. They slowed and stopped on the other side of the door, and I then heard a very gentle knock, three hesitant little raps, immediately followed by Uwe's voice, cautious, concerned, interrogative: "Is everything all right?" he asked.

"I'm here!" I cried, "I'm here!" and then I fell silent. My response must have satisfied him, because after a moment I heard his footfalls receding down the hallway. I tiptoed back to the door and stood leaning against the wall, listening. Uwe might have retraced his steps as well, might also have been listening on the other side of the wall, standing outside the door in the hallway, now and then turning around to transmit little signs of ignorance and impotence toward Inge in the living room. I don't know. I went and sat down on the edge of the tub to consider the situation. When I'd looked out the little dormer a few moments before, I'd realized that it was possible to reach the kitchen by climbing out the bathroom window. In principle, this presented no danger, since the distance between the two windowsills was less than a meter, with a drainpipe running along the facade to cling to as you crossed the divide, and even a little railing to clutch once you'd made it across. The question was whether the kitchen window was unlocked. I opened the little bathroom window again, and, kneeling on the toilet tank, reaching into the open air, I exerted a slight pressure on the glass of the kitchen window, which finally opened. Immediately clambering onto the tank, I climbed out the bathroom window and found myself standing before the void on the window ledge. Pressed to the wall, clutching the drainpipe with both hands, I stood motionless, daring to go neither forward nor back (I'd furtively glanced toward my feet and glimpsed the courtyard below me, the trash cans lined up in a row). In my current position, however, it really wasn't measurably more difficult to go forward than back, and finally I took a half-step sideways to cross over the little meter of

JEAN-PHILIPPE TOUSSAINT

emptiness that separated me from the kitchen window, stopping myself at the last minute from putting my foot into a terra-cotta pot on the windowsill, in which, I noticed as I passed, lay a few shriveled remnants of parsley and basil that hadn't been watered all summer long (and this would once again be my fault: it must be said that I hadn't been around here since the beginning of summer).

I straddled the little railing and leapt into the kitchen, hurriedly dusting off my stomach and thighs. Then, wasting no time, I stealthily advanced toward the refrigerator, soundlessly opened the door, took out the fern, and set it down beside the sink. I brushed a quick, carefree hand through the fronds to give them a bit more volume and shape, like the finishing touch to a stylish coiffure or arrangement of flowers; next I dug up the soil around the stem, in the same manner, hastily scratching and working the peat with my finger, and then I heard footsteps in the hallway. I scarcely had time to turn around and hide my hands behind my back before Uwe entered the kitchen, asking me once again if everything was all right. I explained that I'd taken the liberty of coming and washing my hands in the kitchen after using the toilet. Pensively nodding, he asked if I wanted a towel. "No, no, you're very kind," I told him, "but there's no need." I smiled at him, standing my ground, my hands still behind my back, discreetly rubbing my fingers together to get rid of the last compromising traces of dirt still clinging to them from my quick tilling. My shoulders must have been moving ever so slightly, and Uwe stared at me fixedly, trying to guess what on earth I was up to. He went to pour a glass of water from the faucet, and, as I moved aside to make room, he discovered the fern pot on the drainboard. He glanced at it distractedly as he filled his glass. Then, having no doubt observed that it wasn't where it belonged, he picked it up to carry it back into the living room.

We'd just left the kitchen to make our way back into the living room when Uwe, the fern pot in his hand, disappeared for a moment to go to the bathroom, or at least tried to, but the door wouldn't open, and he couldn't get in. He went on trying to open the door, his hand on the knob, pushing a little harder, but he still couldn't get it to open. I'd stopped in the hallway, watching him. How very strange. I asked if he wanted my help, if he'd like me to hold the fern for a minute. He handed me the pot, and, bending down for a moment to inspect the bolt and the strike-plate, he pushed the knob once again, to no avail. "Do you want me to try?" I asked, handing back the pot, and I tried to open the door in my turn, grasping the doorknob, lifting up slightly, and giving the door a good, sharp push, but it was no use, the door wouldn't open. "It seems to be locked," I said. I knocked very gently. "Is anyone there?" I said. No answer. Uwe was looking at me. "But you were in there just now?" he said. "Yes, but not anymore, as you see," I said. The things he said, sometimes. After a moment Inge joined us in the hallway; having been apprised of the situation, she too tried to open the door, standing sideways with respect to the jamb. Laying one hand flat on the door panel and the other on the knob, clenching her jaws, she gave it a sharp upward push, but didn't get any further than we had. "That's incredible," she said. "Right, well, I'll be on my way," I said. "You're leaving?" she said. "Yes, I'll let you unpack in peace," I said.

Sitting at home reading one August evening a few weeks later, I got a phone call from John Dory, who wanted to know if I had any plans for the next morning. A friend of his, one of his students, had invited him on a little airplane tour of the Berlin skies, and John was wondering if I might like to come along. The girl, he explained, a very nice student of French who also did karate (John had a way of meeting the most unlikely people wherever he went), had a pilot's license and was prepared to take two passengers in her Cessna, or her Piper, he wasn't sure which. We could fly the next day if we wanted, weather permitting. I accepted with pleasure, and arranged to meet John the next morning on the platform of the Alexanderplatz S-Bahn station. Waking up the next morning, I went through all the usual motions, exactly as if I were going to sit down to work. I ate breakfast listening to the seven o'clock news on the radio, and when, already dressed and about to leave, I stepped into my study to get a few things and saw the magnificent light of the sunrise pouring over my desk and raking the floor of the room, I felt a sudden twinge of regret at the thought of having to forgo my work for the day. Truth to tell, it was always this way: the less I thought myself obligated to work, and indeed the more certain the impossibility of working, the more desire to work I felt, and the more capable of working, as if, with the prospect of work receding into the distance, the task shed all its potential torments, simultaneously draping itself in all the many promises of future accomplishment. Thoughtful, I left the apartment, and, heading downstairs with a light heart, I continued to reflect in this same vein, thinking of my work as some delicious, distant eventuality, a bit vague and abstract, reassuring, which only certain circumstances, alas, were temporarily preventing me from seeing through.

I found John on the platform of the Alexanderplatz S-Bahn station, and, after a forty-five minute trip through the Berlin suburbs in the last car of an old subway train, red and cream and virtually empty, we got off at the M. station. There was only one employee on the deserted platform, slowly making his way back to his cabin, his red flag and his walkie-talkie in his hand. We exited the station and found ourselves in the middle of an immense avenue of distinctly Muscovite appearance, with clusters of uniformly gray apartment buildings standing here and there among the vacant lots. There wasn't a human being for several kilometers around, not a newsstand, not a shop, not a café, not a school. Not a cat, not a skinhead. Nothing. Electrical cables stretched away into the infinite distance, joining together at the horizon, on either side of the one tram line that passed through this immense, utterly deserted urban wasteland. Every fifty meters or so the avenue was intersected at right angles by little paved alleyways that led into the apartment buildings' rigorously restricted parking lots, where a small number of cars sat parked dutifully side by side this Sunday morning. Together John and I set off down the sidewalk of that immense deserted avenue, heading eastward, we thought, or northeast (in a quarter of an hour we would be in Rostock, in twenty minutes Vladivostok), stopping at every intersection to try to figure out where we were. Finally we discovered the Rilkestrasse. Reaching the end of this Rilkestrasse—a simple dead-end alleyway that also led to the stellar void of the Gargarin Allee—we began looking around for building D, home to John's student Ursula, wandering randomly from one building to another, first together, John and I, side by side, then separately, each of us venturing off on our own among the identical concrete towers, differentiated only by the occasional faded grayish letter stenciled next to the front door, a ghostly E, the last erratic traces of a half-vanished F. Finally, skirting a row of trash cans lined up in a courtyard, I came across the last legible traces of a D (here we were, Champollion). I called out to John, and together we made our way through the doorless concrete opening that formed the building's entrance, crossing over the threshold, sidestepping some boards set up in a herringbone pattern that blocked our way, avoiding the various detritus on the floor, pieces of wood, crushed beer cans marinating in sinister, stomach-turning puddles of urine and beer. The long row of mailboxes had been pulled from the wall and lay face down on the floor, with one last box still clinging to the wall, alone and abandoned, overflowing with mail, ads, and flyers that someone continued to stuff into it, as if to force-feed it with advertising. We looked around us, slightly dismayed. There were no names on the mailboxes, no list of residents, no manager's office, neither hide nor hair of a concierge. Fortunately John had written down all the details on his little piece of paper, and he told me that Ursula lived on the fourth floor, apartment 438. We opened a door and entered the stairwell, a vast bare concrete shaft pierced at regular intervals by narrow slits overlooking the parking lot, and we climbed the stairs one behind the other, unable to hold back a smile (nice place this Ursula lives in).

On the fourth floor, we found an undamaged door, almost new, with a peephole, and briefly scrutinized the name pasted up over the bell: Schweinfurth. Yes, Schweinfurth, this was the place. Schweinfurth was the girl's name. John rang the bell. A moment later we heard footsteps in the apartment. A boy of fourteen or fifteen in a tracksuit and thick speckled gray socks, young Schweinfurth I suppose, opened the door and led us into a dark interior, telling us to wait in the dining room, a wallpapered space with a pretty waxed wooden table, clear plastic slipcovers on the chairs, a large glass-fronted cabinet holding a collection of miniature folkloric dolls, empty miniature liquor bottles, and a few embroidered place mats. A little further on, in the adjoining living room, two people dressed in bathrobes and slippers were watching television in the dim gray light, scarcely raising their eyes as we came in. The living-room curtains were almost completely closed, and only one milky ray of light entered from outside, its drab colorlessness mingling with the luminous, quivering spectrum emitted by the television set. John and I waited patiently in the dining room, staring at the floor or the ceiling, approaching the glazed cabinet for a look at the dolls. The apartment smelled of frying butter and sourness, sweat, warm track-suits. The boy, no doubt Ursula's brother, had gone off to find his sister in her room ("Die Franzosen!" he'd shouted down the hallway), and the woman watching television in the living room, undoubtedly their mother, had turned around to examine us. We smiled at her, nodding hello from a distance. Very polite, at least, these French officers, she must have been thinking. Rearranging her blue synthetic muslin bathrobe over her breast (eager not to make too bad an impression on her daughter's friends, most likely), she looked at us again and asked if we might like a cup of coffee while we waited for Ursula. Rather than politely declining her offer and continuing to wait quietly in the dining room with the dolls, the incorrigible John accepted with pleasure, unable as always to resist the call of society and its sociable ways; turning around, he quickly tacked toward the living room, entering as if it were the most natural thing in the world and approaching the television. Never removing his eyes from the screen, he let himself sink gently onto the arm of the couch next to Mr. Schweinfurth, who turned and examined him for a moment in surprise. After a minute I went and joined John, entering the living room in my turn, discreetly and soundlessly, as one enters a chapel during services. I discreetly passed by Mr. Schweinfurth, slipping between his knees and the coffee table to make my way toward a chair slightly off to one side, and, sitting down and folding my hands under my chin, I began to watch a documentary interspersing archival footage and recent interviews with railway workers (it had now been more than a month since I'd stopped watching television).

After a moment, Madame Schweinfurth reappeared with the coffee. On a pale blue plastic tray ornamented with a pastel-colored reproduction of a still life stood a thermos bottle wrapped in its tartan, a slightly deformed carton of milk, some sugar, a box of cookies, and a scattered handful of teaspoons. Unmatched and disparate, the coffee service was composed of two red plastic cups, of the tooth-mug style, two others of cream-colored plastic, and one elegant porcelain coffee-cup that I began to covet vaguely as I leaned over the table to make room for Madame Schweinfurth's tray. Thanking me with a glance, Madame Schweinfurth unscrewed the top of the thermos and began serving the coffee, first for John and me (in the tooth-mugs), then for her husband (in the lovely cup I'd been coveting), pouring out equal proportions of coffee and milk, allowing us to add the sugar ourselves, everyone having his own age-old little habits in that regard. I watched her do this (that old woman who can't have been much more than, oh, forty-five). Once everyone had been served, Madame Schweinfurth went and sat down, carefully pulling her dressing gown over her thighs and breast, and sedately lifted her gaze to the television. We held our tooth-mugs in our hands, and no one in the living room spoke. Even the railway-workers had fallen silent (Monsieur Schweinfurth had changed the channel, and found us a good little film on Sat 1).

Ever the thoughtful hostess, very much the lady of the house, Madame Schweinfurth looked at us from time to time to be sure there was nothing we needed, offered us a cookie, refilled our cups. I stood up from the couch to take a cookie from the large tin box she was holding out to me, and, blinking my thanks, I gave her a sheepish smile. Then, still smiling at each other politely, we began nodding our heads pensively; finally, having run out of arguments, a vestige of a smile still hovering on our lips as a sign of our former beatitude, we turned away to take refuge in the less perilous contemplation of the television screen. Once I'd finished my coffee, I set my tooth-mug down on the plastic tray, leaned discreetly toward John, and quietly asked if he was sure this was where Ursula lived. Because otherwise maybe it was time we were going (I'd finished my coffee). Sitting impassive on the arm of the couch with one eye glued to the screen, John reached into his jacket pocket and pulled out the little paper with Ursula's address. He held it up to me with a resigned air: Ursula, Rilkestrasse 14, Blok D, Wohnung 438. Finally I rose (I was beginning to feel a bit fed up with all this), took a few steps through the living room, picked up an old television magazine abandoned on a piece of furniture, and began to leaf through it. Standing next to the window, I absentmindedly flipped through the pages and stopped for a moment on that day's schedule to see what we were watching. There we are, *Malibu*. Mit David Hasselhof (Mitch Buchanon), Alexandra Paul (Stephanie Holden), Pamela D. Anderson (C. J. Parker), Nicole Eggert (Summer Quinn), Kelly Slater (Jimmy Slade), David Charvet (Matt Brody), Gregory Alan-Williams (Garner Ellerbee), Richard Jaeckel (Ben Edwards), Susan Anton (Jackie Quinn). Now this was a doubly intelligent way of watching television, I thought: not only enjoying a deeper knowledge of your chosen program, but also not watching it.

I closed the magazine and put it back where I'd found it, then strode back to the living-room window to await Ursula's arrival. An old mattress stood propped up against a wall in the deserted court-yard below me; a little further on, an abandoned bicycle was lean-ing against the front of a high-voltage box whose concrete surface had been patched with cement slug-trails, waiting to be repainted in a more academic style. Across the way stood a block of apartment buildings, so close that you could see the televisions in the various living rooms. I looked at all those televisions glowing in the little metal frames of the windows; I could even see fairly clearly what the people in those apartments were watching, those who were watch-ing the same series as we were and those who'd chosen another, the ones watching aerobics and the ones watching Sunday Mass, the ones watching cyclo-cross and the ones who'd chosen a home shopping program, and I reflected with dismay that it was a Sunday morning, that it was only a little after nine, and that it was a beautiful day.

And it was then, still distractedly watching those glowing televisions in the windows of the building across the way, that I was struck by the presence of a television glowing all alone in a deserted living room, with no human presence visible before it, a phantom television in a sense, disseminating images in the emp-tiness of a sordid living room on the fourth floor of the building across the way, with an old gray couch half visible in the dimness. The television was showing the same American series we ourselves were watching in the Schweinfurth's living room, such that, as I stood at the window, the image and the sound of the American series reached me simultaneously, but from two different sources, stereophonically in a way, the image before me, tiny and distant on the big bulging screen of the television on the fourth floor of the building across the way, and the sound behind, resounding in the Schweinfurth's living room. After a moment I shifted my gaze to another window, and the sound behind me didn't change, I still had the same German-dubbed voices of the American series in my ears (Monsieur Schweinfurth controlled the remote, and I had no intention of trying to strip him of his scepter), but to the sound thus imposed on me I realized I could adjoin any picture I liked and create whatever program I wished, I had only to let my gaze drift from window to window to change the channel, stopping for a moment on one program or another, such-and-such a series or such-and-such a film. My eyes and ears thus disconnected by these perfectly contradictory programs, I continued to change channels, letting my gaze wander over the windows of the building across the way, more or less mechanically, passing from one screen to the next with a simple sweep of my pupils over the facade, and I reflected that this really was exactly how television presents the world to us every day: speciously, enjoyable only if we give up three of the five senses we ordinarily use to see it as it is.

Finally I heard a noise in the hallway, and Ursula appeared in the living room. I let go of the curtain and turned toward her. She might have been about twenty, barefoot, a hard look in her eyes, her black hair short and unstyled. She stood for a minute before me in the living room, her face down, her eyes on the TV screen.

She wasn't fully awake yet, and her face was still bleary with sleep. Finally she yawned and slowly pivoted in the living room, stretching one arm. "You want some coffee, Ursula?" asked her mother. "No, no, I'm flying," she said. "No stimulants." She was wearing a pair of black leather pants and a white tank top with astonishingly thin straps, her dark nipples discernible underneath. From across the room, I briefly looked at her breasts, her nipples erect under the fine fabric, and felt slightly moved; then, not knowing where to look, I let my gaze wander distractedly through the living room, and finally sat down and began watching television again (in penance).

No one spoke in the car on the way to the airport. Ursula drove silently, wearing an aviator jacket with an upturned sheepskin collar, yawning from time to time, while John, sitting next to her, absentmindedly inspected the contents of the glove compartment: a bag of loose tobacco, a few navigation maps, a pair of thick wool socks rolled into a ball. Finally he dug up a newspaper and spread it out before him on the seat with an expression of intense pleasure, his shoulder briefly shaken by a shudder of well-being (even in a car, John could find some way to read, I wonder if he'd thought of bringing a book to read on the plane). For nearly half an hour we'd been driving down a deserted country road, all trace of urban architecture far behind us, immense beet-fields stretching out on either side of us. From time to time we passed by a distant tractor, a couple of farmers crossing the road with a heavy draft horse, and I was beginning to wonder where we were going, if the landing field was still in Germany (but in Germany it most certainly was, very much in Germany indeed).

A military airbase under the Nazis, a secret military zone in the days of the Soviets, its massive forms suddenly appeared around a bend in the road, surrounded by a wall of rough stone topped with strands of barbed wire and nests of razor wire, with guard towers every ten meters or so. A silent little road led to the main entrance, protected by an electrified gate with a cross-bar and signs forbidding access in several languages, in Russian, in German. When the car stopped at the checkpoint, Ursula rolled down her window halfway to show the guard the laminated ID card from her flying club, bearing her photograph, duly stamped, and we heard what must have been ten wolfhounds locked up in cages barking ferociously, beside themselves with rage, furiously throwing themselves against the bars in hopes of battering them down. A vaguely uniformed, somewhat slovenly young man in canvas boots and a military jacket approached and bent down by the window, accompanied by a dog that continually lunged this way and that, straining at its leash. The guard looked inside the car, and examined us with a disagreeable inquisitorial look. "They're friends of mine," said Ursula, designating us with her upraised chin. Hearing her voice, the dog began to bark and leap at the car, and the guard was on the point of shutting it up with a taste of his canvas boots. He went and casually opened the gate, flashing Ursula a charming smile, drunken and toothless, as she drove through the checkpoint.

We drove slowly through a forest of signs, some strictly limiting our speed to thirty kilometers per hour, others more omi-
nously forbidding access to such and such a building under penalty
of electrocution. Onward we drove through a deserted expanse,
surrounded by the ghosts of SS men and Soviet officers and the
crumbling ruins of various military buildings, rotting and damp,
decrepit, crawling with vermin, the windows broken, exposed to
the weather, traces of brown and green camouflage paint still clinging to the walls, old barracks and canteens, Nazi officers' mess hall,
staff headquarters of the Soviet command. An overturned MiG lay
in the grass, streamlined and sharp, a great broken bird kneeling
on the ground, one wing bent in two, abandoned in the middle
of an alleyway along with the wreckage of several tarp-covered
trucks and a forsaken electrical generator. Everything was silent,
apart from a few little birds chirping here and there. Slowly we
continued toward the main runway, slowing down still further, almost to a crawl, as we jolted over a crude level crossing. The tracks
came to an end on our right, after running through the middle of a
massive brick porch, gloomy and isolated, leading to nothing. We
drove a few hundred meters further through the grounds of the
camp. Still more sordid huts lined the alleyways, more disaffected
bunkers, collapsed pillboxes, piles of rocks and greenery, weeds
and broken stones, interspersed with various abandoned pieces
of corroded metal, valves, a chromed undercarriage, two rusted
exhaust pipes. It was then, still silently making our way through
the grounds, that we turned a corner and suddenly came to the
runways: dozens of kilometers of deserted land, a line of trees in

the distance, studded with signal lights and red and white flags flapping in the wind, the main runway cutting across the field from east to west. One little control tower was kept up for the two or three tourist planes that took off from here on the weekends, and radar antennas turned inexorably on the roof of this little edifice, a windowed three-floor tower whose upper floor could be reached by a steep metal staircase winding circularly around the outside.

We drove slowly onto the runway and continued over the empty tarmac for a few hundred meters. Finally we stopped before a desolate hangar where a man stood waiting by the door, watching us come to a stop. Ursula got out to greet him, and we saw her take off her gloves to shake his hand, exchanging a few words with him as we emerged from the car. Ursula introduced us to Safet, the mechanic, a man of about forty, somewhat grimy and bloated. He shook our hands and picked up his greasy rag. We entered the hangar behind him, walking in single file among the dim silhouettes of various military aircraft, some of them looming over us, a huge bomber, a fighter plane, several helicopters, an old fire truck with its long ladder rising into the shadows, some jeeps, a Soviet ambulance. At the far end of the hangar, among several other more modest crafts, we stopped before a tiny tourist plane, its white wings covered with canvas, the cockpit's glass canopy raised, with yellow and black adhesive strips glued to the wings.

Safet asked us to lend him a hand getting the airplane out of the hangar. Relatively light, maybe six to seven hundred kilos, the plane glided along on the cushion of its tires with scarcely a squeak, you hardly had to push at all, a pleasure in which I didn't indulge to excess; soon I was simply walking alongside the craft, one hand in my pocket, the other confidently resting on one wing like a stable boy's guiding hand on the neck of his horse. Soon the plane sat immobilized on the runway, and Ursula took her place at the controls as I settled in behind her (in the instructor's seat); meanwhile, Safet opened the hood and began fiddling with the motor, his rag in his hand, pushing on the pump lever and holding up a cable with one finger. John stood behind him to watch, his hands behind his back, not unlike a foreman, not unconcerned (Safet seemed to know what he was doing, thank heaven). Once this little operation was over, Safet helped John hoist himself onto the wing of the plane. John's heart was clearly in his boots, and I watched him crawl toward us, an anxious smile on his face (that's how poets are, of course, less at home with the tangible than with the eva-nescent). After a moment he too managed to squeeze himself into the cabin—first thrusting his long legs inside, then twisting as his upper body followed, finally letting himself drop heavily into the seat—and so we sat, perfectly still, realizing what an impossibly cramped little place this was. Ursula pulled down the canopy, and, in total silence, in the profound darkness of the cockpit, amid the glowing lights on the dashboard, the dials of the altimeter and the airspeed indicator, she switched on the ignition. The plane lurched forward, starting off slowly, then stopping again at the end of the runway. I watched Ursula's serious, focused face in a rearview mirror as she went through the final engine checks, her gestures confident and precise. She pressed on a throttle, released a lever, adjusted the trim on a handwheel under her seat. Then, buckling her seat belt, severely cinching the four harness straps over her breast, she turned around for a moment as if to check that there was still someone behind her (yes, yes, I was still there); once she'd been given clearance for takeoff, she turned briskly to John and said she was ready, we were going to take off now. She opened the throttle flat out, and after a brief moment of stillness the airplane began picking up speed, the countryside rolling by faster and faster around us, the airplane shaking every which way, the fuselage vibrating, the canopy jerking upwards over our heads. Ursula gave the joystick a smooth, gentle pull, and the airplane lifted off. We were off the ground, the airplane still vibrating and struggling a bit to stabilize itself as it came out of the climb. I looked straight ahead, my hands clutching John's seat as the airplane swayed left and right, still not quite managing to balance itself; immobile and helpless in the back seat, I vigorously pressed my feet to the floor to retain some sensation of terra firma. Once the plane had finally stabilized, I turned to look groundward behind me, but the runways and control tower of the airfield were already out of sight.

Now the ascent was over, and slowly we flew toward Berlin amid the regular drone of the engines. I looked at the vast sky before me, almost white, translucent, very faintly tinged with blue. We flew over peaceful countryside, it was a beautiful day, a few shreds of summer cumulus hung in the air. Below us I could make out the regular green and yellow squares of the fields, and soon the

outskirts of Berlin began to appear in the distance, the huge con-
centrations of dull gray apartment towers, with scattered touches
of green in the Friedrichshain housing projects. Seen from an altitude of three or four hundred feet, the huge city, far too vast to be
taken in with one glance, appeared as a surprisingly flat and regular
surface, as if crushed by our height, evened out: a simple agglom-
eration of regular blocks in the east, only a little more varied and
wooded in the west, an accumulation of similar quadrilaterals,
sometimes pierced by a wide artery where tiny cars seemed to be
rolling along in slow motion. Sitting in the back of the plane as it
sped fluidly through the sky, I looked at the various monuments
whose distinctive forms were emerging below me, the Siegessäule,
isolated in the center of its star of virtually empty avenues, or the
massive Reichstag, its stone black with soot, a handful of people
playing soccer before it, absurd little silhouettes chasing a ball over
the grass on the esplanade. Further on, past the Brandenburg gate,
not far from the Potsdamerstrasse bridge, I spotted the metallic,
gilded forms of the Philharmonie and the Stattsbibliothek, like
broken kites, like the rigging of ships run aground on the banks of
the Spree. I went on letting my gaze slide over the roofs of the apartment buildings below us, the warehouses and factories, the vast,
desolate vacant lots, the highways and train tracks, the bridges,
the soccer fields and tennis courts of the residential districts, and,
in this assemblage of towers and parks, I occasionally caught sight
of an outdoor pool with hundreds of bathers lying on the grass enjoying the sunshine, a child in a swimsuit standing with one hand
over his eyes, waving at us as we passed by, while Ursula, sitting at

the controls, her gaze sharp and steady under her aviator's helmet, gently began to bank the plane into a broad U-turn. I looked at all those streets and avenues below me, all those houses and apartment towers, those whole districts of Berlin so perfectly delimited by their neighbors, and what struck me most, as we now turned northward, once again flying low over the canal of the Spree, was the incredible number of work sites you could see all over the city. Everywhere you looked there were holes and construction projects, gutted avenues, buildings going up, cranes and mechanical shovels, metal barricades, palisades, all this in varying stages of completion, a simple gigantic hole where a foundation was being laid, a network of metal stalks sunk into a concrete footing, or a superstructure already rising from the ground, a second floor taking shape, burgeoning, halted in mid-emergence, a simple, basic framework, heavy and skeletal, a pure carcass of concrete without doors or windows, a few sheets of transparent plastic over the openings, fluttering in the wind. The work sites were deserted, abandoned, the immense yellow and orange cranes at rest in their palisaded enclosures this Sunday morning, the trucks parked on the sandy slopes of the excavations, the little temporary cabins locked up (there was only the occasional passer-by, enjoying his day off, peering through the cracks in the boards to see how the work was progressing).

We were flying along at a fairly low altitude, and suddenly we found ourselves almost exactly level with the television tower on the Alexanderplatz, fifty meters at most over its summit, which

a blinking red light silently designated to passing planes. Leaning closer to the canopy, I looked at the tower's tall, slender form
as we slowly wheeled around it, this being apparently one of the
landmarks Ursula had been planning to reach before turning back.
I examined the huge metal ball, shining and silvery, and topped
with a giant looming TV transmitter. I'm not sure if the transmitter was still operational, but I scarcely had time to consider that
question before, without warning, Ursula abruptly tilted the plane
to one side and went into a nose dive toward the river. The curve
of our downward trajectory grew steeper and steeper, and we virtually strafed the Palace of the Republic, just over the heads of the
few passers-by strolling on the square, suddenly looking up at us,
Marx and Engels imperturbable on their bronze pedestals; then,
coming out of a 180-degree turn, the airplane accelerating at full
throttle and climbing straight up toward the top of the tower, we
suddenly saw a handful of faces, dumbfounded for a tenth of a second to find us speeding toward them at 210 kilometers per hour,
until, at the last possible moment, Ursula nudged the plane to one
side and glided past the picture windows of the panoramic restaurant, giving us a fleeting glimpse of the few couples sitting inside
at their tables, drinking coffee on the other side of the glass.

Crammed in the back of the plane, my legs squeezed in before
me, my tibias pressed against the canvas back of the pilot's seat, I'd
now chosen to stop looking outside. I kept my eyes fixed on Ursula's
shoulder, on the upturned fleece collar of her aviator jacket, or
on various wildly-spinning hands on the altimeter or tachometer

dials. John had turned around in his seat to see if everything was all right, his long hair billowing with every turbulent little puff of wind that came into the cockpit; he shouted something I couldn't make out in the roar of the wind and the engines, then raised his thumb toward me in a gesture as delighted as it was entangled in the flaps of his jacket and scarf, strapped down and squeezed in as he was. He turned around and looked outside again, his gaze pensive, shining with a mix of ineffable impishness and inner serenity, and when he turned around once again to look into my eyes, seeking a tacit confirmation that we'd just narrowly avoided disaster, I realized for the first time, indisputably, seeing him there before me in the Berlin sky, that, as much in his shining eyes as in the perfectly enigmatic smile lingering a bit too long on his lips, as much in his serenely posed body as in the features that seemed to appear fleetingly on his face, he looked a bit like the Mona Lisa.

The following week I decided to visit the Dahlem Museum. I hadn't been to the Dahlem for several months, and I always enjoyed strolling through the old wooden rooms of the painting gallery, sometimes stopping before a canvas to think, sitting down on a bench and daydreaming a bit, lost in contemplation. At first I permitted myself these little pauses purely for the sake of a few moments' rest but before long I began to enjoy them strictly for their own sake, and nowadays it wasn't unusual for me to head straight for a bench and sit down the moment I walked into a museum. With a painting before me, generally alone, I could sit peacefully for hours and meditate on my monograph, little disturbed by the muffled waltz of the guards silently circling behind me. Sometimes I pulled a notebook from my pocket and took some notes, jotting down a few words in perfect tranquillity as if I were in the quietest library, or at the pool (all that was missing were the goggles on my forehead). I remember many delightful hours spent this way in the Salle des États at the Louvre, for example, sitting all alone on the big velvet bench in the middle of the room, as if in a grounded barque on a lake of precious marquetry. Sitting there on the bench, one hand on the worn velvet seat, I let myself drift along the current of my thoughts as I gazed at some Titian hung from the very topmost rail, turning my back to the *Wedding at Cana* and its empty effervescence, its incessant parade of comings and goings, the unending roil of tourists having their picture taken among the guests.

Before they were regrouped in a new museum in the Tiergarten, the city of Berlin's main painting collections were exhibited in a department of the great Dahlem museographic complex, in a large flat building with smoked-glass windows, whose design and materials, whose vast empty impersonal spaces, whose lobby and staircases seemed more reminiscent of the home office of an international organization than an art museum. The Painting Department was housed in the oldest wing of the building, cohabiting with the Museum of Asiatic Art and some other equally somber and shadowy roommates, the Museum of Indian Art, the Museum of Islamic Art, the Ethnographic Museum (in whose dimly-lit interior you sometimes came face to face with the fragile, tired form of a pre-Colombian figure). Every time I'd been to the Dahlem, since I used the main museum entrance rather than the separate door for the Painting Department, I'd always come across some of those pre-Colombian beauties slumbering in their glass cases on my way in. Never dawdling before these marvels, I hurried straight toward the painting gallery, quickly slipping through a hidden door I knew of at the far end of a room in the Ethnographic Museum; leaving the treasures of several ancient civilizations behind me, I resolutely made my way into the painting galleries, traveling backward down the centuries, headed for the Renaissance, striding unhesitatingly through rooms devoted to French and English painting of the eighteenth century, a long string of Nattiers, Bouchers, Largillierres, Hoppners, and Raeburns, at which I cast a rapid glance as I passed, taking care not to judge them. Because, it seems to me, however peremptory one may be in one's admiration, one must remain modest in denigration. We must not make a virtue of ignorance, in other words, or misunderstanding, or the inability to be charmed or to love (now there was a thought that did me proud, I told myself, hurrying past all that crap as quick as I could).

That morning, then, after a frugal working breakfast with myself, I left my apartment early to head for the museum. Arriving at the Dahlem, feeling some false hunger pangs, I bought myself a sandwich at an Imbiss by the bus stop. I gave my sandwich a quick once-over (it was no bargain). There was a little bun, open on one side like an *in-octavo*, with an impasto of butter and a slice of desiccated, oily Gouda, warped, rectangular, and oversized, emerging from the bread like a bookmark. I didn't have time to eat it before I reached the museum; I only had a moment, scarcely enough for one little bite. I contented myself with a few nibbles at the emerging Gouda as I walked. Lithely, I climbed the front staircase and bought a ticket at the window. My sandwich still in my hand, wondering what to do with it now, taking one last bite and then pacing circularly through the lobby in a vain search for a trash can, momentarily considering putting it in my jacket pocket but realizing it wouldn't fit unless I slipped it in upright, which for my dignity's sake I preferred to avoid, not to mention that it might have soiled my notebooks, I decided to give up and enter the museum with my sandwich (I couldn't very well check my sandwich at the cloakroom).

I strode slowly down the great entry hall and glanced into the shop where they sold art books and postcards. Two or three people stood before the bins, flipping through the volumes with a leisurely finger, as in a secondhand bookstore. Continuing on through a few more doorways, I entered the Painting Department, walked through several rooms, and descended a flight of steps into the Dürer gallery, where I was greeted by an odor of old wood and wax. Silent and empty, the Dürer room was lined with dark wooden panels, long rays of sunlight streaming through two big barred windows and layering the air with a gentle, golden light, muted and spangled. I soundlessly crossed the room with my sandwich to make for the bench; sitting down in that mild, library-like chiaroscuro, all shadowy corners and great splashes of light on the walls, I began to work quietly on my monograph as if in the most peaceful of all retreats. The adjoining room had been closed for renovations earlier in the summer, and even blocked off with a little chain, meaning that the only way to reach me was through the room next door, Room 137, where no one ever went, obviously (unless they had some interest in the Master of the Old Retable of the Holy Kinship). Alone in the Dürer room, my rear flank protected, in a sort of secluded private study deep within the museum, I could let my ideas run free. I looked at the paintings, and various thoughts began flooding into my mind, slowly combining and dispersing like currents in the ocean waters, and from all these irregular pulses coursing through my neurons, from that disorder, that internal chaos, came a feeling of plenitude and a sense of coherence. I'd set my hat and my sandwich beside me on the bench, the sandwich on a paper napkin whose edges I pulled up from time to time, for decency's sake, as a painter protects Eve's modesty with a wisp of diaphanous tulle; but the napkin's edges always fell limply back onto the bench, inevitably leaving the sandwich naked beside me.

I'd been sitting in the Dürer room for some ten minutes when a man entered, his gait slow, very tall, elegant, white-haired, with a polka-dot handkerchief matching his tie. Without a glance in my direction, he slowly strode toward the portrait of Jerome Holzschuher and looked at it for a moment, his hands behind his back; then, moving on to the next painting with great self-assurance—

you could see he was well acquainted with the art of strolling through rooms in museums—he stopped in front of the largest Dürer in the room, the *Madonna with a Siskin*, where he stood pensive and still for some time, his hands joined and his gaze fixed, his pupil intense, before taking a few steps back to come and sit down on the bench, briefly looking behind him to see where he was about to sit as I hurriedly pulled my hat from under his buttocks (fleetingly saying to myself: please don't let him sit on my sandwich). The man came and sat down, next to the sandwich thank God, giving it a sidelong glance as if there were a turd lying there between us, then looking up at me in surprise and proceeding to a brief, attentive scrutiny of my person. A little uncomfortable, my eyes resolutely fixed on the portrait of Jerome Holzschuher, I studiously considered the canvas, pulled a notebook from my pocket, opened it, and began paging through it distractedly. Giving the sandwich another dubious glance and raising his eyes once more to me, he silently left the room, the echo of his footfalls following him in decrescendo through the adjoining rooms.

Pensively, I closed my notebook and put it back in my jacket pocket. I owned a whole collection of notebooks, notepads, and scratchpads made by Rhodia or Schleicher & Schuell, with orange covers and detachable pages, as well as several little square Chinese notebooks with elegant hard covers in black and red. I always took a few of these with me when I went out, slipping them into my pocket before leaving my study, gradually filling them with bits or fragments of sentences, thoughts and aphorisms, observations and remarks (the latter being generally only the more accurate expression of the next-to-latter), which as a rule I never made use of in my actual work. No matter how brilliant, an idea really wasn't worth keeping if you couldn't even remember it without writing it down, it seemed to me. Besides, whenever I opened one of those notebooks as I lay on my bed or sat at my desk, paging through it a bit, happily lingering over the few drawings or pencil sketches I'd scratched out here and there, I inevitably found nothing particularly interesting in all those pages I'd methodically filled up day after day; so wonderfully luminous when they first came to me, so feverishly scrawled down, my ideas now seemed sadly faded, their ink dried, their perfume blown away. Viewed with detachment, with neither enthusiasm nor disgust, their effect on me was more or less that of my underpants when I stuffed them into a plastic bag before heading off to the laundry room: only a vague, familiar affection, rooted more in the memory of a brief moment of communion than in any real objective merit.

Now I stood up, taking my sandwich, and approached the portrait of Jerome Holzschuher for one last look before I went on my way. I leaned in toward the bottom of the canvas to inspect a detail, and suddenly a guard called out to me from the doorway and wordlessly waved me away. I straightened up a bit and shot him a questioning glance, though without really taking my eyes off the painting. He stood in the doorway, red and corpulent in his regulation gray suit. Never moving from his spot, he went on slowly waving me back, his fingers joined, warning me away from the painting. Paying him no mind, but backing up a few centimeters all the same, I resumed my scrutiny of the canvas, and, as I once again leaned a bit closer, the guard suddenly came stalking toward me, shouting to get away from the painting. "Yes, yes," I said, getting away from the painting ("Try not to shout," I added, "remember you're speaking German, for goodness' sake"). This little scene might have grown still more heated if he hadn't just then received a crackling, inarticulate service call on his walkie-talkie. Calming down a bit, answering his colleague on the other end, staring at me darkly all the while, he told me again, more civilly (he must have taken me for a tourist) that I did not have the right to get so close to the paintings. Yes, so I'd gathered.

I went downstairs to the cafeteria and took a seat at a table next to a picture window that looked onto a tranquil little garden, where a worker in green coveralls was collecting stray trash, nudging it into an empty basket with a rake and a shovel. There were about ten of us in the cafeteria at that late-morning hour, all sitting at separate tables. I'd ordered a cappuccino, and I was glancing through a catalog in the sunlight when, not far away, I heard a succession of little barks, or rather squeals, groans of animal pleasure. Intrigued by these sounds, I turned and looked around to see where they might be coming from. A few tables away sat an aged esthete, innocent as a pope, in a lilac-colored shirt and a cardigan, a jasmine scarf knotted around his neck, reading the newspaper with a cup of tea on the table before him, occasionally casting a paternal glance at his two miniature poodles, identical and coiffed, their flanks shorn like ewes and their quivering tails topped with a pompom. He'd tied their leashes to the foot of his table, and the two poodles were continually going after each other, tangling their leashes in their frenzy to mount one another, the one insistently trying to bugger the other, the other forever fleeing under the table. These two little lechers were called Cassis and Myosotis, as I learned from their master's mouth, when, after a placid sip of tea, he bent down to try to calm his little proteges' ardor (and not Prime Time and Dream Team, nor even, more mimetically, as I'd also imagined with a smile as I watched them frolicking under the table, Sodom and No More).

Leaving the cafeteria to go back to the museum, I walked down a long windowed corridor and found myself before a very heavy door, with an articulated arm to make it swing shut automatically. Somewhat hesitant, I pushed it open and entered a dim hallway, then climbed a few steps beside a little concrete ramp for the carts that traveled the museum's service passageways. I walked a few meters further, occasionally turning around to look behind me, and ended up in a boiler room. The far end lay shrouded in darkness, the walls and ceiling covered with tubes of various sizes, some thick, round, and elbowed like water-heater conduits, others slender and copper, running straight down the length of the room, studded here and there with control valves, meters, and pressure indicators. Various extinguishers were fixed to the walls, along with other sorts of fire-fighting equipment, basic and diverse, fat tan canvas fire hoses rolled up on spools, oxygen tanks and masks, even a stretcher leaning upright against the wall. I turned around and retraced my steps back down the hallway, the boiler's low, rumbling murmur behind me; trying to find the door I'd come in by, I turned into a narrow concrete corridor lit by pallid fluorescent lights. Here, every ten meters or so, I saw a series of disturbing armored boxes, presumably high-voltage, their doors emblazoned with explicit expressionistic pictograms, stylized black lightning bolts and stricken, contorted men, frozen in an asymmetric fall. I must have made a wrong turn (or else the restrooms were very poorly marked). I still hadn't met a living soul since leaving the cafeteria. Climbing a dim little staircase in search of the way back to the museum, I spotted a windowed guard room where two hallways met, empty, a jacket draped over the back of a chair and a newspaper abandoned on a table. High on the walls, rows of video monitors were broadcasting images from the various rooms of the museum one floor above, dense black and white overhead views, badly framed and a bit out of focus, like something from an underground parking garage, virtually impossible to make out. I paused before the glass wall of that deserted outpost and looked at the gray screens before me. Every now and then, you could see a visitor slowly coming and going in one of the painting galleries overhead, silently making his way across the fuzzy screen, leaving a very faint trail of himself in his wake, then merging with himself and gradually re-entering his corporeal envelope when he stopped before a painting. The paintings themselves were indiscernible on those rows of monitors bolted to the guardroom wall, too small to show up on the screens, for one thing, but also washed out by the brilliant sunlight flooding the rooms. Nevertheless, after studying the monitors for some time, I finally recognized a painting that had been a starting point for my study, the portrait of Emperor Charles V by Christoph Amberger.

It was impossible to make out Charles V on the screen, of course, and I wasn't sure how much of my recognition came from my direct observation and how much from my prior knowledge of the canvas, far more reliable and precise. I shut my eyes, and, as I stood in that empty hallway in the basement of the Dahlem Museum, Charles V slowly appeared behind my closed eyelids. There he was in his wooden frame, his body slightly bent forward, his hands almost touching at the bottom of the canvas, gazing straight ahead with calm self-assurance, his chin covered by a light beard, very fine, almost impalpable, like downy fuzz. His face was smooth and young—he was still an adolescent, he who then reigned over an empire—his cheeks and forehead pale, almost white, the skin slightly scaly, the painting çrazed in places, the varnish cracked, tiny fissures visible on the very surface of his face. I opened my eyes, and when my gaze landed on the screen again what I saw was the reflection of my own face, slowly surfacing from the electronic limbo of the monitor's depths.

Heading homeward after the museum, I decided to round out my workday with a swim. I went straight to the pool and pushed on the door, but found it stubbornly closed and unwilling to budge.

A long, undulating tremor even ran upwards through the glass under the vain pressure of my hand. I leaned closer for a look inside, my hand above my eyes, and saw the lobby abandoned and empty in the darkness, the closed-up front desk and the massive forms of the automatic ticket machines half-visible in the dimness, as well as a number of cork bulletin boards with private ads and official notices tacked to them. I could vaguely make out the pool in the distance, drained of its water. Two workers in blue coveralls were walking along the bottom, their feet bare and their pant legs rolled up, slowly descending the slope where a mosaic of white and azure porcelain tiles depicted the gigantic form of an impassive Poseidon, a trident in one hand, lying flat on the floor amid a small crowd of tritons. I watched the two workers advancing over the god's face with their brushes and hoses, scrubbing his beard and rubbing his eyes with their mops. Slowly, a tide of dirty, foaming water washed down the slope and disappeared into the grate-covered drains at the pool's four corners. Undiscouraged by this little setback, I immediately headed off for another pool I knew of, less intimate but no less agreeable, although it was far larger, more crowded, and noisier, like the Sainte-Geneviève Library, for example, compared to the cozy and delicious little Forney Library on the Rue du Figuier. Even the locker room was different, in one case a simple dusky vestibule, often deserted and silent, with two neatly aligned rows of lockers, a place to undress and pull on your swimming gear in perfect quietude, in the other a vast brightly-lit concourse with endless ranges of metal lockers, full of clamor and traffic, bathers and puddles. I changed into my swimsuit and, fleeing the tumult of the showers, headed for the pool with my towel over my shoulder. Rinsing my feet under a poolside faucet, I laid my towel on a chaise-longue along with my work notebooks and a felt-tip pen and prudently entered the water, carefully settling my goggles on my forehead (right, let's get to work).

I swam slowly through the clear water, my goggles on my forehead, smoothly veering to one side now and then to avoid contact with some particularly erratic young swimmer. I didn't feel entirely at home in these virtually unknown waters, and so, lacking my usual reference points, I couldn't abandon myself to my studies as wholly as in my usual pool. Not only was I forced to keep a vigilant eye on the many careless and unmethodical swimmers around me, but I also lacked the instinctive spatial awareness I enjoyed in my usual pool, thanks to which my gaze could immediately and unerringly locate the big wall chronometer that revealed my intermediary lap time, for instance, or one of the various smaller black and white clocks that, without interrupting my train of thought, without in any way disrupting the ideas I was forming, instantly told me how long I'd been in the water, and thus how long I'd been working. Still, even if the work conditions weren't as ideal as they were at my usual pool, I nevertheless spent an agreeable moment there in the water. Studious and focused, my goggles on my forehead, I swam tranquilly, letting my gaze wander around me. Across the pool, not far from the entrance to the women's locker room, I saw a row of unpainted wooden sauna cabins in which one could have oneself irradiated for the price of a few coins, something like hermetic little individual shower stalls, emitting a powerful fluorescent-violet glow, perfectly silent and sinister. I went on swimming my lengths at my own speed, casting an occasional glance toward those grim cabins, whose doors I could see opening and closing at regular intervals according to a ritual that to some extent escaped me, and suddenly I had the impression I was seeing a sort of life-size recreation of *The Fountain of Youth*, that big, wonderful Cranach displayed at the Dahlem, which shows a parade of decrepit old women entering the waters of a basin and emerging from the other side as fresh young girls, except that in this case it was young women going into the shower stalls, with long hair and one-piece bathing suits, their thighs firm and their stomachs flat, carefully laying their towels on the little wooden benches before closing the cabin door to strip off (sometimes, glancing under the door as I continued my lengths, I could even see a swimsuit slipping furtively over an ankle, which then gracefully rose from the floor), and it was old women who emerged when I looked up again a few moments later, at the end of another length, very tan, their thin legs wobbling unsteadily as they walked, the skin on their necks desiccated, their décolleté hollow and bony and speckled with liver spots, towels in their hands, some of them in bathing caps, beneath which there might still be a few sparse strands of hair, white, thin, wiry, and no doubt stubbornly resistant to the metallic torments of the teeth of their combs, baldness and its miseries presumably being the principal drawback of these repeated irradiations, which did on the other hand give them a fine telegenic tint. Now I'd once again come to the end of the pool, and I set off back toward the other side with a supple propulsive thrust of the toes, but I'd scarcely taken one stroke before I collided flabbily with another swimmer, floating on his back with a little red foam board under his nape. Embarrassed to have been the cause of this accident, he quickly raised a woeful head from the board to offer his excuses (*mì*! it was Mechelius!).

Mechelius and I lifted ourselves out of the water and sat down on the edge of the pool, not far from the beautiful rounded silvery banisters of the metal ladder by which we'd emerged. We sat dabbling our feet in the water, as in the baths of yesteryear, side by side, two Roman senators, myself in a swimsuit by Speedo, with the little white stylized-boomerang logo on the loin, my swimming goggles on my forehead, him in ample boxer-style trunks, rumpled and damp and clinging to his thighs, his locker key knotted around his wrist. His nose was running a little, his lips bluish, as if bruised, and trembling with cold. Melancholy, eyes downcast, he explained that his doctor had advised daily aquatic exercise for his bad back; then, lowering his voice, he went on to confide that he'd been concerned for his health ever since he'd seen the very troubling results of some medical tests he'd undergone. He even confessed, under the seal of secrecy, that he was planning to retire from the foundation, judging that the moment to pass the torch might have come, the time to slowly shed his responsibilities and start thinking of a successor. I nodded pensively, having little to contribute (imagine if I now had to see to Mechelius's successor, on top of everything else), but this sudden intrusion of Mechelius's

TELEVISION

private life into my work (because I at least was working, I don't
know if he realized he was interrupting my work), along with his
health problems, his thoughts of retirement, and his melancholy,
was becoming a bit much to bear, and, without warning, I abruptly
slipped into the water, holding my nose, and let myself sink motionless to the bottom.

A moment later I returned to his side, pulling myself onto the
rim of the pool, first placing one knee on the concrete, then haul-
ing the other leg out, painfully, as Mechelius looked on in surprise.
My goal was achieved (I'd completely shut him up), and, settling
in beside him, I carelessly pulled up one side of my swimsuit with
my finger and let it snap sharply against my skin (just showing off).
We resumed our discussion of this and that by the pool, and when
Mechelius, gradually regaining his composure, asked if I'd seen
the TV show a few days before on the Fuggers, the great Augsburg
banking family, and heard me answer no, he explained that he'd
found it a rather interesting program, intelligently constructed,
well-researched, with some good archival material. "No, no, I
didn't see it," I repeated, smoothly stirring the water with my legs
again. I pulled out one foot, inspected it dubiously for a moment,
my leg outstretched, and told him I'd stopped watching television.
"What about you, do you watch a lot of television?" I asked, turning toward him. Reflexively, he stiffened and crossed his arms over
his chest in a defensive and distancing posture (in his gaze I fleetingly read that he thought it really very underhanded to ask such
a question when he'd just compromised himself by talking to me

about a TV show), and immediately protested that he did not. "No, no, very little," he said, "more or less never, maybe an opera now and then, or certain old films. But I tape them," he added, "I tape them" (as if the fact that he taped them might somehow soften the reproach that could be leveled against him for watching them).

I'd often observed this kind of quiet, troubled modesty when people were forced to speak of the relationship we all have with television. They seemed to broach the subject in spite of themselves, as if discussing some grave illness which touched their lives not indirectly but on the most intimate level. Unable to deny their affliction, they strove at least to minimize its consequences, underscoring the frequent respites that the illness still granted them, the happy times when its torments seemed bearable, when its effects seemed to fade, when they could thus lead a normal life, those several evenings a week when they still went out to the theater or a concert, those long Sunday afternoons spent simply reading at home. No doubt this brought them a kind of reassurance, this insistence on the few hours of their lives still spared by the disease, and so they complacently thought their condition less serious than it was, its progression less unstoppable, when in fact the disturbing symptoms were only multiplying: turn to the last pages of any newspaper, and you'll see those thousands of tiny coded bits of information spreading and spreading, invading the columns like infected cells, metastasizing, progressively replacing the ever-weakening healthy cells of the newspapers (some of them, defeated and overrun, were already in the terminal stage); and even out in

the streets, in the cafés, in the buses and subways, on the radio, in
the offices, in every conversation the subject was never anything
other than television, as if the very basis of conversation, its single
visceral material, had become television, and in spite of all this
everyone went on looking away, forever denying the gravity of the
disease (even Titian's initials, I'd suddenly realized, were T.V.).

Delon and the children came back to Berlin at the start of Sep-
tember (the littlest one still flew for free, not having been born yet).
The afternoon of her return, I'd shown up at Tempelhof Airport a
half-hour early and wandered around the airport waiting for their
plane. There was no one in the main arrivals hall, which served as
both a gigantic waiting room and a check-in area for the few de-
parting flights. All the shops were closed, the metal shutters pulled
down over the storefronts, the airline counters deserted, the luggage carousels stilled. I paused to look through the windows of a
closed newsstand, where foreign papers were slumbering on a rack
in the dark. I slowly retraced my steps, my hands in my pockets,
pressed on to the bar, had a cup of coffee standing at the counter,
then went and sat down on one of the innumerable plastic chairs in
the waiting area of the vast empty hall. Finally Delon's plane was
announced, and I rose from my seat to go stand by the doorway
where the arriving passengers would appear. The baggage claim
was in a little room out of sight, and the first passengers were be-

ginning to emerge with their suitcases. I stood on tiptoe and finally spotted Delon in the crowd, pushing a cart loaded with a precarious pile of suitcases and traveling bags, along with a transparent green and red plastic sack from a duty-free shop in Rome Fiumicino. She was very tan, my Delon, and already she was laughing as she came cautiously toward me, one hand on her cart to hold back the bags, in black pants and a white tee-shirt, pregnant, glowing, smiling, looking like a movie star in her dark glasses. My son was walking beside her, and he sprinted forward to embrace me as soon as he spotted me. "We have a present for you!" he announced. "A present," I said, "really?" "Yes, look in there," Delon answered, motioning with her chin toward the big transparent bag from the Fiumicino duty-free shops. I opened it and pulled out a large rectangular cardboard box bearing the word TEATRO in blue-mauve capital letters, diagonally barred as if stamped with some official seal, accompanied by a drawing of an ultrathin black machine: a Goldstar VCR (I dubiously turned the box over and read the words "Made in Germany" in tiny letters on the bottom).

Outside the airport, pushing the baggage cart, I looked around for a taxi. Delon walked beside me, slow, majestic, her head high, her shoulders slightly pulled back. Never losing that air of regal serenity that pregnant women generally display when they're walking beside me, she let her self-assured gaze wander over the airport's parvis, supporting her belly from below with both hands, while her face, her peaceful expression, and her quietly confident gaze expressed her legitimate pride in carrying with her the future of an empire (in this case, our little girl). There was a row of taxis parked a little further on, a dozen or so of those big custard-colored German cars they use as taxicabs in Berlin waiting in single file, and we climbed into the first one we found. I set my son on my knees. He'd been sick on the plane and was preparing to be sick again in the taxi, his face ashen, little beads of sweat beginning to form along his hairline. Beside me Delon looked out the window, smiling behind her sunglasses. I took her hand, and, stealing a glance at her face, I observed a few traces of light ocher powder on her cheek, which moved me to scoot closer for a surreptitious sniff of her skin and her hair, taking in the scent of cosmetics, freshness, and musk that emanated from her face.

Back at home, we set about unpacking the bags in the bedroom. The suitcases were scattered haphazardly over the floor, the biggest one lying open on the bed, with several sweaters and a pair of socks spilling out. Unhurried, chatting, we went back and forth from suitcase to armoire, hanging up the clothes one by one on their hangers while my son looked on, lying on the bed, lazily wriggling his feet and demanding that I come play a game of ice-hockey in the living room ("Have a heart, Daddy," he kept saying, "have a heart"). "Oh, all right already," I finally surrendered, once the suitcase was empty, and I accompanied him down the hallway into the living room. "Go guard the goal," I told him, taking off my shoes. Oh, my legs were so stiff, so very stiff. And me not even forty yet. Such dreadful prospects I had before me. "No, you be the goalie," he said. I told him I was willing to play, but not as goalie.

I was forty years old, after all. Not far from forty, anyway, and after all that's an age when it's much more fun to skate fancy-free through the living room in your socks than to stand in the goal and expose yourself to your son's potshots. My son was sulking. Theatrically, he crossed his arms over his chest; he didn't want to play anymore. I stood waiting in my socks, holding my stick. "Oh, all right, I'll play goalie," I said (I was doing this mostly for his sake). I liked hockey too, I won't deny it, but I wouldn't have been playing if it weren't for him. "Can we turn on the TV?" he asked. "No, it's broken," I said. He shot me a mistrustful look. Disinclined to be played for a fool, like Saint Thomas, or like a good Jesuit, he wanted to see for himself. He headed over toward the set, and he would surely have turned it on if I hadn't urgently come forward, skating along in my socks, and stopped his hand at the last minute. "What did I say?" I said. I looked at him severely. It was time I regained the upper hand. "Come on, get into the goal," I said. He didn't dare protest. I set the puck on the floor, sent it sliding over the parquet with my stick, skated left, right, dodged my son as he launched himself at my knees, caught myself on one leg, staggered, pivoted, shot, scored. "Goal! See that?" I said. "Your son's a sieve," I said to Delon, skating through the living room to resume my position in mid-rink. "Let him win, he's five years old!" she said, sitting down facing us on the couch. "Five years old already!" I said (it was incredible how that changed all the time: just fifteen pages ago, he was four and a half). "At the rate you're writing, he'll be an adult before you're in print," Delon told me.

After the match, a bit winded, my forehead slightly damp with perspiration, I went and sat down on the couch next to Delon. I put on my shoes and tied them neatly. After a moment, my son joined us on the couch and scooted over the cushion toward me. "We have a present for you," he whispered into my ear. "Yes, I know, the VCR," I said. "Can we turn it on?" he said. "No, it's broken," I told him. "It's broken too?" he exclaimed incredulously, and, kneeling on the couch, he grasped his head with both hands in an attitude of despair, as if he'd just missed a penalty shot. "It is indeed," I said, spreading my arms. "I'm sorry." He must have thought we were really amazingly unlucky with electronics, and he set off toward his room, his head down, grumpily kicking a Lego as he passed. Delon stood up and went to turn on some music in the next room. She came back into the living room, dancing on tiptoe, weaving through the room in her bare feet, her arms making slow, vaguely Arabian arabesques. Languidly, in the spirit of the Khaled song on the stereo, she stepped up onto the couch, swaying her hips and looking into my eyes, her shoulders still, her arms outstretched and undulating from side to side, her hips still swaying sensuously to the rhythm of the music, and she smiled at me as she performed a belly dance made all the more voluptuous by the fact that she was six months pregnant.

That evening I took a bath after dinner. I lay on my back in the bathtub, listening to the slow movement of Beethoven's sixteenth and last string quartet. I lay perfectly still, only a little less active than the musicians playing beside me, their bows almost motionless on the strings, like my hands and my arms, which I sometimes imperceptibly shifted in the water alongside my thigh. I'd set a white saucer on the rim of the bathtub, with a candle fixed into its own dried wax, and all around me, in the darkness of the bathroom, the oblong little flame vacillated, outstretched and orange, two or three centimeters high, with a tiny incandescent dot at the top of the wick. The light hung motionless around me, and I watched the flame stretching and sinking in the room like the music itself, which occasionally curved in on itself, sank down and then soared upwards, hovering suspended in the air. After a while, Delon came into the bathroom and sat down beside me on a stool. I took one hand out of the water, and, placing it gently on her thighs, asked if she wanted to go to bed.

Back in the bedroom, we'd made love (I'll say no more than that: there are times when it's best to let the delights of action prevail over the pleasures of description). Delon was lying naked on the bed beside me, her stomach still in the half-light, and I looked at the smooth, stretched skin around her navel, and her head inclined to one side, her eyes staring into mine with an incredibly direct and confident gaze. I took her hand and squeezed it tenderly.

The next morning, after breakfast, I went off to take Babelon to school. We'd found him a kindergarten as soon as we'd moved to Berlin, and in general it was my job to take him to school. Every day, we ritually took a seat on the bus's upper deck and watched the streets of Berlin parade past before us, side by side in the first row of the *impériale*, my son serious and concentrated with his backpack and his padded leatherette hunter's cap, now and then rising from his seat to pretend he was driving, an imaginary steering wheel before him, which he spun like the great wheel of a ship there on the upper floor of the bus. My son had immediately taken to his new life in Berlin; it was a joy to see how quickly he bonded with his new teachers and established dozens of complicated little rapports with the other children at school, worldly and clannish as children are at that age, four years, four and a half, I'm not quite sure anymore how old my son might have been at that point (he was six now). Leaving the house that morning, we'd gone to catch the bus on the Arnheim-platz, and, spurning several buses that had "just one floor," as my son disdainfully put it—thereby signifying that, where Berlin buses were concerned, two floors were the norm and one an exception, a strange and vaguely disagreeable anomaly—we'd climbed into an impeccable 104 and made straight for the *impériale* (the ideal spot, obviously, for thinking of Charles V).

The Charlottenburg neighborhood, home to my son's kinder-garten, was the heart of the huge Russian community that took root in Berlin at the beginning of the twenties; they used to call it Charlottengrad in the days before the war. There was nothing left now of the network of cafés and little restaurants that once surrounded the Stuttgarter Platz, bistros and art galleries, tiny basement bookshops where people must have come to play chess in the steam of the samovars and the smell of the books. Rather, the area along the Kantstrasse now teemed with discount shops selling cut-rate electronics, catering mostly to border-dwelling Poles who came to Berlin by the busload to stock up. Often, crossing the street to take my son to school in the morning, I would meet several bands of such men pushing stripped-down shopping carts they'd converted into private freight wagons, filled to the brim with cardboard boxes holding transistor radios and radio alarm clocks, clocks and calculators, stereo speakers and VCRs, heading back toward the waiting buses under the railway bridge. There, in the rumbling darkness of the bridge's looming stone arch, they began unwrapping their purchases to leave more room in the luggage compartment, while a wary driver looked on, sucking at a cigarette as he stood some distance away by the buses, indescribable old hulks, decrepit and grimy, with broad grilled radiators below the hoods and dingy little flowered curtains hanging limply at the windows.

That morning, after leaving my son at his school, I decided to stick around the neighborhood for a while and stroll through the streets by the railway bridge. I had nothing in particular to do, and I slowly walked up Kantstrasse toward the Savignyplatz, looking in the windows of the electronics shops. As a rule, the merchandise sat piled haphazardly in boxes in the shop windows. Here and there, star-shaped tags had been stuck to the glass doors, announcing fabulous deals: eight Panasonic televisions for two-thousand-nine-hundred-ninety-nine marks. In the window of one of these shops, dusty and run-down, falsely resembling an authentic avant-garde art gallery, thirteen standard televisions were displayed in classical style, like some youthful work by Paik or Vostell. I stopped and looked at the glowing screens, with no deflection animating them, no sound pulsating them, no magnet deforming them, or widening them, or corkscrewing them, or sweeping them, or shrinking them, nothing, no synthesizer, no spiral, no ellipse, no form, no soul, no movement, no idea, only the same image thirteen times over, a host in a studio at 9:15 in the morning (on one of the sets, a frame line kept sweeping relentlessly over the poor sap's face). Pensive, I went on my way, stopping again before another electronics shop a few meters further on, this one very modern, with a big blue neon sign blinking in the street. Behind the glass lay a vast selection of VCRs and video cameras, and I gazed for a while at the different models of TV sets, black and gray with elegant dark glints, like gleaming sedans. Hesitating, hanging around the shop window for some time, looking every inch the prowler, I finally made up my mind and entered the shop. A salesman serenely stepped out from behind the counter and strode forward at a jaunty clip, tugging at his cuffs with an expectant half-smile, his two agile hands even now eager to make themselves useful. "Can I help you?" he asked amiably.

In the taxi that took me back home, the big TV box on my knees, I looked out the window, broodingly watching the streets of Berlin roll by (I'd been seduced by a little portable number).

JEAN-PHILIPPE TOUSSAINT

Back in the apartment, finding that Delon had gone out, I went into the bedroom, hurriedly took the TV from its box, and set it on a chair to surprise her when she came home. I turned it on. It began to hiss, displaying a snowy screen that must evoke the first or last seconds of the universe's existence, and I started it scanning through the frequencies to set the various channels. With the remote in my hand, I wandered through the great void that was the absence of programs, astral and vaguely disturbing; whenever a new image appeared on the screen, I assigned it to the selected channel, referring to the eighteen-language instruction booklet that came with the set. This done, I quickly ran through all the channels I'd stored in the TV's memory, taking in a little global view of the varied, multicolored bouquet I'd put together for Delon. Just because I myself had stopped watching television, that didn't mean I had to deprive Delon as well, it seemed to me (but since, from another angle, I absolutely insisted that the living-room television no longer be used, I'd finally resigned myself to this compromise). I fine-tuned the settings a bit, adjusted the contrast, brightened the color. There, that was fine, everything was in order. I turned off the set and headed into my study to get back to work.

The moral: since I'd stopped watching television, we had two TVs.

That evening, as Delon lay in bed watching television, I installed my son before a cartoon in the living room. Given that the set in the living room now served no purpose (even the antenna had been disconnected), I'd consented after some pleading to let it occasionally act as a video monitor so my son could watch his cassettes on the VCR Delon had brought back from Italy for him. As for me, I'd withdrawn to my study to work, surrounded on both sides by the sound of a TV or video-monitor speaker, penetrating the walls, endlessly disturbing the thoughts I was trying to develop. For several minutes, various parasitical bits of information had been surfacing in my brain and melding with my own thoughts, and my mind struggled to concentrate even as it was absorbing the top stories of the eight o'clock news on German channel 1 and the bellicose expostulations of the French-dubbed Robin Hood in my son's cartoon. Finally I stood up, a little put out, and went into the living room to make my son turn down the sound. Stretched out on the couch in his little red and white cotton pyjamas, my son watched me enter, unmoving (fatalistically, as one contemplates a passing storm), watching his cartoon, his mouth agape, his knees level with his face, dreamily twiddling his wang and his nuts inside his pyjama bottoms. My appearance seemed not to deter him in the slightest; he only glanced up for a moment to see who was coming in, then looked back toward the screen, still doing as he pleased in his pyjama bottoms. "What's the matter, you got an itchy wiener, or what?" I asked him. "No, why?" he said. I turned down the sound on the monitor and left the room (he reminded me of me, sometimes).

Back in my study, I sat down at my desk again, but no sooner had I returned to my thoughts than I heard a scream from the bedroom. "Come here! Come see!" Delon was shouting. I hurried out of the study and raced toward the bedroom. What was going on? Was she in labor? Had her water broken? No, no. Delon greeted me calmly, a pen in her hand and a dictionary open before her, queenly and lascivious in her bed, amid a chaos of papers and letters, open notebooks and folders, a cup of tea, little cookie wrappers with serrated ruffs lying majestically on the sheets like water lilies afloat on a lake of rumpled covers. "Quick, look," she said, pointing at the television. I bent down before the set and found myself nose to nose with my upstairs neighbor, Uwe Drescher (Guy), who was participating in a televised debate. "Come here," Delon said, "come and sit down," she said to me, delighted, making room next to her on the bed, and she explained that she'd happened onto Uwe as she was flipping through the channels. I took a few steps backward and sat down on the bed. There was Uwe before me on the screen, with his ruddy face and his scholarly little glasses, representing his party in a roundtable on the city. Together Delon and I watched the debate for a few minutes, listening as Uwe expressed himself with aplomb, exchanging amused and complicitous smiles on the bed, agreeing that he really made an excellent representative, if not of his party, then at least of our building.

I went back to work in my study, still hearing the muted music of *Robin Hood* on my right, and, on my left, slightly muffled as it passed through the walls, a few quiet echoes of Uwe's roundtable on the city, when I realized I was hearing another murmur in the study, still more muffled, coming neither from the living room nor from the bedroom. What now? I bent an attentive ear, and, rising from my chair, I stood up and took a few steps, staring at the ceiling, examining the ornamental grooves and friezes. Struck by an idea, wanting to find out for sure, I took off my shoes and climbed onto my director's chair. Standing there in my socks, my eyes closed, my ear trained on the ceiling, I summoned up all my auditory might, and, just as I thought, it really was a television I was hearing, one floor above me, not directly over my head but in the Dreschers' bedroom, where I imagine Inge must also have been watching her husband on TV.

This was too much. I put my son to bed (after watching the end of *Robin Hood* with him in the living room, distractedly paging through a book as I sat on one arm of the couch), then went back to the bedroom and lay down. I stuffed a pillow behind my back and began reading quietly on the bed. From time to time I interrupted my reading to cast a careless glance toward the television screen, where Uwe's roundtable was still going on. Then, seeing that Uwe himself had the floor, I lay my book down on my thighs to follow the debate for a moment, vaguely listening to what was being said. Delon had stopped watching television long before, and she lay with her head on my shoulder. She took my right hand and put it on her bare stomach, lifting the covers. "Can you feel her moving?" she asked quietly. "She almost always starts moving when I lie still like this for a minute." My hand lay on Delon's stomach, and all at once I did indeed feel something like the waves of a tiny electric current propagating under my fingers, the skin on Delon's stomach bulging very slightly under the pressure of an invisible foot or shoulder that must have been moving inside her belly.

After a while, Delon went to sleep. I looked at her lying beside me in the bed, her cheek on the pillow, her shoulder bare, her eyes closed. Gently taking my hand from her stomach, I turned off the bedside light on her nightstand. Now the bedroom was dark, except for the milky glow from the television on the chair. I leaned over Delon to pick up the remote control she'd dropped on the covers beside her, and I quickly flipped through the channels again, watching the images parade past on the screen, all the films, all the panel discussions, all the commercials. Then I aimed the remote at the set and turned off the television. I leaned back against my pillow and sat for a long time in the dark, not moving, simply savoring that little moment of eternity: silence and darkness regained.

The fictional worlds that Jean-Philippe Toussaint creates are pleasantly quirky ones, worlds where hopelessly benighted humans struggle with the small vexations of everyday life and where those struggles, described in lavish (and indeed obsessive) detail, gradually assume the proportions of an epic. His heroes are anonymous figures, men without qualities who seek moments of peace in an existence where the simplest of situations inevitably go awry in unpredictable, capricious ways. The tales he tells are comic ones, without a doubt. Yet our laughter may be leavened by the sobering recognition that, despite their apparent strangeness, Toussaint's worlds resemble our own world far too closely.

The French critic Jean-Louis Ezine, writing in the *Nouvel Observateur,* called Toussaint "the most imaginative writer of his generation." Such praise is all the more impressive in view of the fact that Toussaint's generation includes a number of writers—Jean Echenoz, Marie NDiaye, Christian Oster, Jacques Jouet, Lydie Salvayre, Eric Chevillard, Marie Redonnet, and Christian Gailly, to name just a few—who have reconfigured the fundamental principles of the French novel and who have launched that cultural form on a variety of promising new trajectories.

Toussaint's own trajectory, in the seven novels he has written since inaugurating his career in 1985, is perhaps more earthbound. He is interested in the landscape of the quotidian. Or, more specifically, in the details of ordinary life that most novelists take for granted and that are consequently passed over without comment in their work. Toussaint's alchemical gesture consists of an intense focus upon the everyday, in order to persuade us that, contrary to everything we have learned and assumed, trivial concerns are in fact richly evocative and worthy of our interest. Thus, his protagonists approach the small tasks of daily life with the kind of trepidation that a more traditional sort of hero might feel upon entering the gates of hell. And indeed, they will encounter rare adventure where more conventional folk would find only ennui.

The narrator of Toussaint's first novel, *The Bathroom,* has seemingly renounced the world—or has at least reduced its dimensions to those of his bathroom, having decided to spend as much time as he possibly can in his bathtub. Yet, like Oblomov on his couch, he fails to find there the kind of ataraxia that he seeks. The hero of his second novel is a businessman, but one would be hard-pressed to say just what his business is. At the office, he has perfected the art of doing nothing whatsoever, and he has become such a virtuoso in that art that his colleagues recognize in his inanition the sign of a truly devoted worker. Another of Toussaint's protagonists leads a life so bereft of interest that the high point of his existence is a pedicure in Milan. Yet another manages to travel to Japan, but when he tries to speak German with the people he meets there, they do not understand him. In short, Toussaint's heroes are *idiots.* And I mean that in the noblest sense of that word: they are recumbent, quietist, befuddled, overmatched, and largely taciturn figures who are, finally and inescapably, quite utterly themselves. As such, they might lay claim to a venerable lineage in our cultural history, appropriating the legacy of precursors such as Peter Schlemiel, Bartleby, Prince Myshkin, Gregor Samsa, Zeno, the Good Soldier Schweik, Walter Mitty, and Portnoy, for example. They choose, rather, to slouch through life as best they can on their own terms, relying on their own dubious resources, grappling with dilemmas largely of their own creation. We watch them from a safe distance, as their gropings, hesitations, and false starts carnivalize our own efforts to come to terms with the real.

The hero of *Television* takes his place in Toussaint's bumbling fraternity with some degree of brio, for he has made a very courageous decision: he has resolved to stop watching television (as soon as the Tour de France is over, that is). Television, he realizes, has taken over his life in insidious ways. It has made him a spectator, rather than a doer; he has become indifferent under its influence; he has no time left to reflect, since he has invested all of his meager powers in an empty gaze. Yet even as he flees from it, television and its simulacra pursue him everywhere he goes. Video surveillance screens in a museum mock him, as do microfiche machines in a library. Gazing out the window of an apartment building in Berlin, he realizes that every other person in that neighborhood is watching television—and they are all tuned, with nauseating inevitability, to *Baywatch*. Paging through the newspaper in front of his own (now-darkened) TV screen, he finds himself reading the television guide.

Supposedly, at least, he is a man of the written word, an academic who has taken a sabbatical year in Berlin in order to write a study of Titian. Yet even the initial letters of his subject's name, Tiziano Vecellio, inscribe the name of his nemesis, writ large. Staring into his own computer screen (yet another simulacrum of TV), he realizes that after several months of work on his project, he has written only two words, "When Musset." He tells himself that not writing is at least as important as writing and that all good things will finally come to those who wait. He is a first-class rationalizer, a casuist of rare accomplishment, and a truly gifted procrastinator. Anyone who has indulged those guilty pleasures (however infrequently) will recognize in him a master practitioner.

As richly comic as this novel may be, it is not without seriousness of purpose. For as he chronicles his hero's addiction to TV, Toussaint also points toward the addiction of the society in which he lives. Television's dominion in that society's aesthetics is nigh absolute, Toussaint argues. That leaves very little room for the written word—whether it be a question of a treatise on Titian or a novel. While the competition between television and the narrator's treatise plays itself out, it gradually becomes clear that Jean-Philippe Toussaint may be directing our attention to a far broader agonistic pitched on a much vaster stage. For as much as anything else, *Television* is about the ways in which novels compete for our attention with other, newer media, in an increasingly unequal duel where some of the most basic terms of our culture hang breathlessly in the balance. And the real hero of *that* struggle, Toussaint suggests, is the novel itself.

—Warren Motte
2004

COLEMAN DOWELL SERIES

The Coleman Dowell Series is made possible through a generous contribution by an anonymous donor. This endowed contribution allows Dalkey Archive Press to publish one book a year in this series.

Born in Kentucky in 1925, Coleman Dowell moved to New York in 1950 to work in theater and television as a playwright and composer/lyricist, but by age forty turned to writing fiction. His works include *One of the Children Is Crying* (1968), *Mrs. October Was Here* (1974), *Island People* (1976), *Too Much Flesh and Jabez* (1977), and *White on Black on White* (1983). After his death in 1985, *The Houses of Children: Collected Stories* was published in 1987, and his memoir about his theatrical years, *A Star-Bright Lie,* was published in 1993.

Since his death, a number of his books have been reissued in the United States, as well as translated for publication in other countries.

SELECTED DALKEY ARCHIVE PAPERBACKS

FOR A FULL LIST OF PUBLICATIONS, VISIT:
www.dalkeyarchive.com

CAROLE MASO, *AVA.*

LADISLAV MATEJKA AND KRYSTYNA POMORSKA, EDS.,
Readings in Russian Poetics: Formalist and Structuralist Views.

HARRY MATHEWS,
The Case of the Persevering Maltese: Collected Essays.
Cigarettes.
The Conversions.
The Human Country: New and Collected Stories.
The Journalist.
Singular Pleasures.
The Sinking of the Odradek Stadium.
Tlooth.
20 Lines a Day.

ROBERT L. MCLAUGHLIN, ED.,
Innovations: An Anthology of Modern & Contemporary Fiction.

STEVEN MILLHAUSER, *The Barnum Museum.*
In the Penny Arcade.

RALPH J. MILLS, JR., *Essays on Poetry.*

OLIVE MOORE, *Spleen.*

NICHOLAS MOSLEY, *Accident.*
Assassins.
Catastrophe Practice.
Children of Darkness and Light.
The Hesperides Tree.
Hopeful Monsters.
Imago Bird.
Impossible Object.
Inventing God.
Judith.
Natalie Natalia.
Serpent.
The Uses of Slime Mould: Essays of Four Decades.

WARREN F. MOTTE, JR.,
Fables of the Novel: French Fiction since 1990.
Oulipo: A Primer of Potential Literature.

YVES NAVARRE, *Our Share of Time.*

DOROTHY NELSON, *Tar and Feathers.*

WILFRIDO D. NOLLEDO, *But for the Lovers.*

FLANN O'BRIEN, *At Swim-Two-Birds.*
At War.
The Best of Myles.
The Dalkey Archive.
Further Cuttings.
The Hard Life.
The Poor Mouth.
The Third Policeman.

CLAUDE OLLIER, *The Mise-en-Scène.*

FERNANDO DEL PASO, *Palinuro of Mexico.*

ROBERT PINGET, *The Inquisitory.*
Mahu or The Material.

RAYMOND QUENEAU, *The Last Days.*
Odile.
Pierrot Mon Ami.
Saint Glinglin.

ANN QUIN, *Berg.*
Passages.
Three.
Tripticks.

ISHMAEL REED, *The Free-Lance Pallbearers.*
The Last Days of Louisiana Red.
Reckless Eyeballing.
The Terrible Threes.
The Terrible Twos.
Yellow Back Radio Broke-Down.

JULIÁN RÍOS, *Larva: A Midsummer Night's Babel.*
Poundemonium.

AUGUSTO ROA BASTOS, *I the Supreme.*

JACQUES ROUBAUD, *The Great Fire of London.*
Hortense in Exile.
Hortense Is Abducted.
The Plurality of Worlds of Lewis.
The Princess Hoppy.
Some Thing Black.

LEON S. ROUDIEZ, *French Fiction Revisited.*

VEDRANA RUDAN, *Night.*

LUIS RAFAEL SÁNCHEZ, *Macho Camacho's Beat.*

SEVERO SARDUY, *Cobra & Maitreya.*

NATHALIE SARRAUTE, *Do You Hear Them?*
Martereau.

ARNO SCHMIDT, *Collected Stories.*
Nobodaddy's Children.

CHRISTINE SCHUTT, *Nightwork.*

GAIL SCOTT, *My Paris.*

JUNE AKERS SEESE,
Is This What Other Women Feel Too?
What Waiting Really Means.

AURELIE SHEEHAN, *Jack Kerouac Is Pregnant.*

VIKTOR SHKLOVSKY,
A Sentimental Journey: Memoirs 1917-1922.
Theory of Prose.
Third Factory.
Zoo, or Letters Not about Love.

JOSEF ŠKVORECKÝ,
The Engineer of Human Souls.

CLAUDE SIMON, *The Invitation.*

GILBERT SORRENTINO, *Aberration of Starlight.*
Blue Pastoral.
Crystal Vision.
Imaginative Qualities of Actual Things.
Mulligan Stew.
Pack of Lies.
The Sky Changes.
Something Said.
Splendide-Hôtel.
Steelwork.
Under the Shadow.

W. M. SPACKMAN, *The Complete Fiction.*

GERTRUDE STEIN, *Lucy Church Amiably.*
The Making of Americans.
A Novel of Thank You.

PIOTR SZEWC, *Annihilation.*

STEFAN THEMERSON, *Tom Harris.*

JEAN-PHILIPPE TOUSSAINT, *Television.*

ESTHER TUSQUETS, *Stranded.*

DUBRAVKA UGRESIC, *Thank You for Not Reading.*

LUISA VALENZUELA, *He Who Searches.*

BORIS VIAN, *Heartsnatcher.*

PAUL WEST, *Words for a Deaf Daughter & Gala.*

CURTIS WHITE, *America's Magic Mountain.*
The Idea of Home.
Memories of My Father Watching TV.
Monstrous Possibility.
Requiem.

DIANE WILLIAMS, *Excitability: Selected Stories.*
Romancer Erector.

DOUGLAS WOOLF, *Wall to Wall.*
Ya! & John-Juan.

PHILIP WYLIE, *Generation of Vipers.*

MARGUERITE YOUNG, *Angel in the Forest.*
Miss MacIntosh, My Darling.

REYOUNG, *Unbabbling.*

LOUIS ZUKOFSKY, *Collected Fiction.*

SCOTT ZWIREN, *God Head.*